About the book

Hello. I'm Alex, and in my spare time, I have b
started out as a story for my teenage daughte. ~~ ·~~~ ~··~ ~··j~y.
But then I got to wondering if I could improve it to the point where other, less nepotistically biased people might enjoy it too.

The story is entirely original by me. It's not based on any existing people or ideas. It is based on a plotline that I've had in my head since I was young too. And I'm glad that I was finally able to complete it.

The genre is Speculative Fiction. I've really enjoyed writing it, and I've learned lots along the way. However, it's difficult to be completely objective about it, especially when you're so close to the story. If you see areas that could be improved, then please get in touch. I would appreciate it. If the suggestions are good, then I will collect them together, update the text in the book, and republish it—i.e., as a "version 2".

You can contact me at: alex@ry-lan.com

I hope you enjoy reading it as much as I enjoyed writing it. Thank you!

Copyright © Alex Rogers 2024
Edited by Brian Cross
Published by Amazon

Ry-Lan

by Alex Rogers

To Eleanor

Chapter 1

Wed 3rd April 2024

Morning mists lingered like final whispers of the night as the sun crested the eastern hills of the Yorkshire Moors. Its rays filtered through the cloud, casting a soft glow and softening the rugged landscape. Alex Harper's police car, a dark blue SUV marked only by the gleaming emblem of the North Yorkshire constabulary, navigated the serpentine roads that ribboned across the expansive moors. Its rugged design was well-suited for the unpredictable terrain, with reinforced suspension and all-terrain tyres whispering against the gravel and mud. The car's powerful headlights pierced the mist, beacons of authority in the remote, windswept terrain.

The Yorkshire Moors, a vast plateau of rolling heather and peat bogs, stretched out in a patchwork of gorse-clad hills and shadow-filled valleys. This morning, like many others, the moors seemed to exist outside of time, relics of an ancient wilderness preserved in the heart of modern Britain. Narrow and infrequently travelled roads wound through quaint villages and past stone cottages dotting the view like relics of a bygone era.

Alex, a man of forty-five with a keen sense of duty etched into his sharp features, drove with practiced ease from years of patrolling this region. His piercing blue eyes mirrored the vast openness of the moors, reflecting a depth often attributed to those who spent their lives in solitude among nature. His morning stubble and slightly unkempt hair suggested a man who prioritised practicality over appearance, a trait that served him well in the rural expanses of North Yorkshire.

That morning, Alex had started his shift with a routine check of the outlying areas of Helmworth, a small market town famed for its medieval church and weekly livestock auctions. He had driven past Lower Helmworth's ancient stone buildings, noting the early risers setting up stalls for the day's market. The air was crisp, carrying the scent of moist earth and faint traces of wood smoke from nearby homes.

As he left the village behind, the countryside opened up, revealing the true expanse of the moors. Alex's route took him past Derwent's Cross, a lonely intersection named after a centuries-old boundary stone marking the meeting point of four ancient sheep trails. From there, he drove through Brackendale, where the hills rose steeply, their slopes covered in dense bracken beginning to turn golden with the approach of autumn.

The moorland was far more than a mere backdrop to Alex's daily routine; it was a steadfast companion. Among these hills, Alex found a sense of home, his life deeply anchored to the rhythmic ebb and flow of the seasons and the enduring dance of the natural world. His bond with the land was shaped not by romantic ideals but by profound respect and understanding cultivated over years of serving its communities and safeguarding its rich heritage. The moors were the one constant in his life, a horizon remaining unchanged as the years and seasons passed.

As Alex rounded a bend, the full panorama of the North Yorkshire Moors opened before him. Here, the land was untamed, dominated by heather stretching to the horizon, interspersed with jagged rocks and the occasional stand of weather-beaten trees. The sky above was a vast dome, now clearing as the last morning mist burned away under a strengthening sun.

This part of his morning patrol was always his favourite, a moment of solitude amidst the moors' vast beauty before the day unfolded with its unpredictable duties. He little suspected that today, something extraordinary would challenge his deep-rooted connection to this land.

* * *

The sharp crackle of the radio pierced the morning's tranquillity. "Control to Sergeant Harper." Shirley's voice carried its normal clarity and composure. "We've received a report from Mr Thompson of Bingley farm. Over."

Alex snatched up the radio handset. "Harper here, go ahead," he responded.

"He reports something unusual on his property. Details are scarce, but he appears quite disturbed. Could you investigate? Over."

"Roger that, on my way. Harper out."

"Tommy" Thompson was known in the community for his level-headedness, which made his current unease all the more alarming.

Alex redirected his vehicle towards the farm. The Bingley farm nestled on the eastern edge of the moors, a scenic route Alex knew well, having patrolled it countless times before. As he drove, the vista transitioned from wild moorland to a more structured farmland environment, where stone walls partitioned off the rolling fields from the untamed heather.

His mind raced with possibilities. Tommy was not one to make a fuss over nothing. The nature of rural police work often involved dealing with unusual situations—from livestock thefts to the occasional lost tourist wandering too far from the hiking trails. Yet, something suggested this was no ordinary call. Alex felt a stir of anticipation; it was not often that something truly out of the ordinary came his way.

As he approached the farm, the imposing silhouette of the Thompson farmhouse came into view, its ancient stones bearing witness to centuries of rural history. The vehicle crunched along the gravel path leading up to the farmyard, disturbing a flock of birds pecking idly at the ground. They flew in a flurry of wings, adding to the sense of something impending.

Tommy stood waiting for him by the gate, his ruddy face unusually pale, his eyes wide and alert. "Alex, thank goodness," he called on Alex's approach. His voice carried a tone bordering on reverence. "After I called about the strange thing in the field, I went back out to take another look — that's when I spotted him lying there beside it. I haven't touched anything, mind you. It's like nothing I've ever seen before, and him, just out cold on the ground like that."

Together, they hastened through the farm, passing the quiet barns and the livestock, now seeming to sense the tension in the air. The usual rural scents of fresh hay and animal musk were there but tinged with a sharper edge, a crispness charged with urgency. An unmistakable sense of the unknown now overshadowed the familiarity of the farm as each step brought them closer to the unsettling discovery awaiting in the field.

As they neared the field in question, Alex's pulse quickened. The description Tommy had been unable to provide over the phone awaited him, promising to be as bizarre as the morning's earlier calm was peaceful. What lay ahead could very well be a routine part of his job, or it might just be the beginning of something far beyond his usual rural police duties.

* * *

The journey through the familiar farm setting had done little to prepare Alex for what awaited. They arrived at a part of the property that Tommy rarely used—a remote pasture bordered by dense thickets of bramble and ancient stone walls overgrown with moss. As they traversed the uneven ground, the reason for Tommy's unease became quickly apparent.

In the middle of the field, a spherical object lay, unlike anything Alex had ever encountered in his years of policing the moors. It was metallic, perfectly smooth, and emitted a faint hum that resonated with the quiet of the surrounding moorland. The sphere was about three metres in diameter, its surface reflecting the overcast sky with almost mirror-like perfection. It looked surreal, as though a piece of a futuristic spacecraft had inexplicably found its way to this forgotten corner of North Yorkshire.

Beside the sphere, a man lay sprawled on the ground, face down, unconscious. His attire caught Alex's attention—it was sleek and form-fitting, made of a fabric shimmering subtly in the morning light, suggesting a high-tech origin. On his shoulder, a name badge adorned with characters was visible. The writing style appeared oriental, though Alex could not determine its exact origin; it was neither Cyrillic nor Latin but something different and enigmatic.

"After I called you about the sphere, I took another look around the field, and that's when I found him here, like this," Tommy whispered, his voice barely audible as if reluctant to disturb the profound silence enveloping the field. "I haven't touched him or it. Been waiting for you to arrive."

Alex's mind raced as he took in the scene. Protocol dictated caution. He quickly pulled out his radio to call for medical assistance, his voice steady, projecting the situation's urgency. "Harper to control. Request immediate ambulance support at Bingley farm. Inform the chief we have an incident involving an unidentified object and a casualty. Urgent assistance required."

While waiting for the emergency services, Alex began a preliminary inspection, careful not to touch the sphere or the unknown man. He circled the object, noting its lack of seams or openings. It was as if the sphere had been crafted from a single, unbroken mould — and materialised whole, right here among the bracken and wildflowers of the Yorkshire scenery.

The unconscious man showed no apparent signs of injury, but his condition was clearly serious. Alex checked for a pulse, relieved to find it strong and steady beneath his fingers. Whatever had happened here, the man was alive but in dire need of medical attention.

As Alex stood up, his gaze returned to the mysterious sphere. It presented a challenge to the normalcy of his daily routine. Its surface was impeccably smooth and reflected the grey sky and green of the surrounding field. The material, whatever it was, seemed to absorb and radiate light simultaneously, giving it an almost ethereal quality.

The sphere's positioning in the otherwise undisturbed field was curious. A line of two indentations led up to where it rested; the first was about ten metres away and shallow, while the second, about 20 metres away, was noticeably deeper. This peculiar pattern suggested the sphere might have bounced to its current location, yet, perplexingly, there were no trails indicating it had rolled across the grass. The lack of any disturbances around it only deepened the mystery of its arrival in Tommy's field.

The quiet hum it emitted was almost calming, yet it underscored the utter strangeness of the circumstances. Alex pulled out his notebook, jotting observations and noting every detail that could help to understand what exactly had landed so quietly yet disruptively in the field. As he wrote, he circled the sphere at a respectful distance, trying to spot any markings or features that were out of view on his first inspection. Every angle provided new reflections but no new answers. It remained inscrutable and immaculate, an alien presence silently making the Yorkshire moors its temporary home.

The ambulance sounded in the distance, its siren contrasting the surreal calm of the scene before him. Alex took a deep breath, steadying himself. He was the first responder, the first to face this mystery, and perhaps the key to unravelling it. As the medical team arrived, bustling into action, Alex's role shifted subtly from caretaker of the public order to guardian of a potential cosmic enigma.

The field, once just a backdrop to the pastoral serenity of rural Yorkshire, was now a stage for a drama seeming to reach far beyond. As he coordinated with the paramedics, Alex focused on the broader implications of his find. What was this sphere? Who was this man? And most importantly, what did their appearance here mean for the safety and security of his community?

* * *

As the paramedics tended to the unconscious man, Alex's attention returned to the object. Despite its otherworldly appearance, his training kicked in, grounding him in procedure and caution. Photographing the object from various angles ensured the images captured its sheen, the surrounding area, and the lack of any marks of impact—a fact that deepened the mystery of its arrival.

"I need to secure this area," Alex announced, his voice carrying an edge of authority. He instructed Tommy to remain behind the police tape he was setting up. "No one goes near this until we understand what it is. That includes the press, locals, and everyone. We don't need rumours starting up."

Tommy assented, his usual jovial demeanour subdued by the morning's events. "Of course, Alex. You'll let me know if there's anything I can do?"

"Absolutely," Alex responded, appreciative of the farmer's cooperation. Then, with the perimeter securely established, he followed protocol by informing his superior about the peculiar occurrence. He pulled out his mobile phone and dialled the chief inspector's office number. The secretary answered the phone promptly.

"Chief inspector's office, how may I help you?"

"Hi, this is Sergeant Harper. I'm currently at Bingley farm where I've encountered an unusual situation. There's an unidentified object and a man unconscious beside it. The man is wearing some kind of uniform, possibly oriental, with writing on it. I've secured the area, and the incident is contained. But I thought it necessary to inform the chief inspector," Alex explained, calmly relaying all relevant details.

"Thank you, Sergeant Harper. The chief inspector is in a meeting at the moment, but I'll make sure your message is relayed as soon as she is available," the secretary assured him.

"Thank you," Alex replied, ending the call. Returning the phone to his pocket, he surveyed the scene again, the sphere and the unconscious man extraordinarily standing out from an otherwise ordinary field. Despite the strange circumstances, Alex felt grounded in his duty, reminded that following procedure was crucial even in the face of the unknown.

The paramedics, well-trained in handling delicate situations, were preparing to transport the unconscious man to the hospital with practiced precision and quiet efficiency. One carefully supported the man's neck to ensure his spine remained aligned, while the other gently lifted his legs.

As they placed the man on the stretcher, they did so with great care, securing him with straps to stabilise his position. A thermal blanket was then unfolded and draped over him to preserve body heat, a critical measure to prevent shock given his unknown condition and the cool breeze sweeping across the moor.

Once securely positioned, the medics wheeled the stretcher towards the waiting ambulance, choosing a path clear of the mysterious sphere. The team's avoidance was not merely procedural but instinctive, reflecting a natural caution given the unexplained circumstances of the man's discovery.

They communicated in low, concise tones, each phrase a testament to their focus and the seriousness of the moment. Reaching the ambulance, they lifted the stretcher with synchronised effort into the vehicle, where various medical equipment awaited. Quickly, they began to assess the man's vital signs, attaching sensors and preparing IV lines with swift, assured motions.

Unanswered questions thickened the air, each medic moving with the weight of the unknown pressing down upon them. As the ambulance doors closed, Alex felt relief and a heavy realisation that the mystery was far from over. The ambulance's engine hummed to life, and with a wave from a medic, the vehicle pulled away, its lights flashing as it disappeared down the winding road.

* * *

With the ambulance gone, Alex returned his attention to the sphere. The field was now quiet; the earlier commotion subdued into a thoughtful silence. He trod the perimeter he had set up, his boots crunching softly on the underbrush, ensuring the tape was secure and visible. A routine task, maybe, yet his mind was anything but still. Each step introduced a new angle and perspective on the gleaming object sitting so incongruously in the middle of the North Yorkshire countryside.

Tommy stood at a respectful distance, his earlier anxiety replaced with a quiet curiosity. "Never seen anything like it, Harper," he said, his voice low, almost reverent. Alex agreed, scanning the sphere's smooth, metallic surface. It offered no answers, only reflecting the cloud-streaked sky above and the green earth around.

"Neither have I, Tommy," Alex replied, his voice carrying awe and caution. "Keep this under wraps for now, yeah? Until we know what we're dealing with."

"Of course," Tommy affirmed, his gaze lingering on the sphere before he turned back towards his farmhouse, leaving Alex alone with his thoughts.

The midday quiet was now fully upon him, the sun in the sky casting short shadows lightly around his feet. Alex took out his notebook again, flipping it open to a new page. He began to jot down his thoughts, not just the observations and facts meticulously noted, but his feelings about the morning's events. Not his usual procedure in the least, but then, nothing about this day was normal.

As he wrote, he contemplated the implications of what the sphere could be. Was it a satellite, a drone, or perhaps something military? Yet none of these possibilities seemed to fit the complete lack of markings, the absence of any visible seams or openings, or the strange, humming vibration permeating the air around it. The more he thought, the more he felt that something truly extraordinary had happened, something that might not just be beyond his experience but perhaps beyond his understanding.

Alex paused, his pen hovering over the paper. He looked around at the sprawling moors and felt the vastness of the sky above and the deep, ancient ground beneath. This sphere, whatever it was, had chosen to appear here in a place timeless and remote. The responsibility of what to do next weighed heavily on him, a testament to the role he played not just as a police officer but as a guardian of these lands.

Alex sighed and closed his notebook. He decided to take a final walk around the perimeter, needing to reassure himself that everything was as secure as possible. As he went, he felt the eyes of the moors on him, the silent, watchful gaze of nature bearing witness to human curiosity and its endless quest for answers.

The day was far from over, and Alex knew the unfolding situation would soon catch his superiors' attention, prompting directives that could change the course of his enquiry. But for now, in this brief lull, he allowed himself a moment just to be—to stand amidst the unfolding mystery and wonder of it all. His mind teemed with questions as he gazed at the silent sphere under the vast Yorkshire sky: What was this object? Where did it come from? And most importantly, what did its presence mean for them all? Prepared for whatever might come next, Alex felt the hand of fate pushing him towards revelations that might alter everything he knew.

Chapter 2

Ninety minutes had passed since the ambulance carrying the unconscious man arrived at the local hospital. The urgency of his condition had ushered him straight into the emergency unit, where he was now under the intensive care of Dr Zayn and his team. As Alex Harper strode through the hospital's sliding doors, the sterile smell of antiseptic washed over him, a marked difference from the earthy air of the Yorkshire Moors that he was so used to.

He approached the reception desk, the hospital's hustle echoing around him. "I'm here to see the man admitted earlier from Bingley farm," he said to the receptionist, who nodded and picked up the phone to alert the attending physician.

A few moments later, Dr Zayn appeared from around the corner. He wasn't expecting Alex, but his face lit up when he saw him. "Sergeant Harper, right?" Dr Zayn extended his hand in greeting. "I heard you were the one who found him. Do you have any more information about our mystery patient?"

Dr Zayn shared what little they knew as they walked towards the secluded observation room where the patient was being cared for. "We're calling him 'Ry-Lan' for now. One of our junior doctors, who is Chinese, recognised the writing on his name badge. It says 'Ry-Lan'. It's helpful, but there's still so much we don't understand."

Inside the room, Ry-Lan lay motionless on a hospital bed, his breathing steady yet unnaturally precise, monitored by a constellation of medical equipment beeping and flashing rhythmically. Dr Zayn paused beside the bed, scanning the array of screens. "We found implants in his central nervous system and compounds in his blood that don't match any known biological materials. It's as if his physiology has been ... engineered."

Alex, absorbing every word, noted the clinical detachment in the doctor's voice, a defence against the baffling reality they were confronting. "Engineered? Are you suggesting he's been modified?" Alex asked, failing to fully take in the implications.

Dr Zayn looked at him. "Modified? Perhaps. We really need to understand where he is from. Can you help us identify him so we can get a bit more detail on what we're dealing with?"

"Yes, of course. We'll make enquiries and get him identified."

As Alex looked down at Ry-Lan, the man's features seemed both human and impossibly precise, an eerie testament to the unknown technology running through his veins. The reality of what lay before him was overwhelming, yet Alex knew this was only the beginning of a deeper, more complex investigation.

"Please keep me updated on any changes in his condition," Alex said, his voice steady despite the turmoil of thoughts. On leaving the observation room, his determination hardened; the sphere, the man, and now these revelations—each was a piece of a puzzle he was more resolved than ever to solve.

* * *

After leaving the hospital, Alex drove back through the winding roads of the Yorkshire Moors, the setting sun casting long shadows over the terrain. The surreal events of the day replayed in his mind, each detail vivid against the backdrop of the familiar yet enigmatic moorland. Upon reaching his modest home nestled on the outskirts of a nearby village, the solitude of his surroundings welcomed him—an echo of his own introspective mood.

Alex didn't bother with the lights as he entered, preferring the dimming twilight filling his living room. He sank into his favourite armchair, the fabric worn by years of similar quiet evenings, though none quite as heavy with thought as this one. The house was silent, save for the occasional creak of settling wood mirroring the quiet contemplation occupying Alex.

That was until his phone rumbled on the coffee table, a glance at the display revealing the caller's identity, his boss, Chief Inspector West.

'Sergeant Harper, I received your initial report on the incident at Bingley farm. I appreciate it's late, but I've been at a meeting. Do you have any update for me?"

Alex repressed a sigh. He'd been expecting a call, just not this late in the day, but then, rumours abounded about the chief's domestic issues. 'The individual involved is an IC1 male aged around thirty. He is currently unconscious but breathing steadily and is being monitored at Helmsworth hospital, Ma'am.'

A pause. 'I see. And what about this unidentified object that he was found next to?' came the tired-sounding voice.

Alex racked his brains for an answer to satisfy his boss, but there simply wasn't one right now. Seconds later, though, came a reprieve. 'Look, I've got to go. I'll leave it in your hands. Just keep me updated.' The CI cut the call, and Alex breathed an audible sigh; CI West's involvement had been waylaid for now.

As he poured himself a small glass of whisky, the amber liquid catching the last light as he swirled it slowly, watching it cling to the sides of the glass, his mind drifted back to Ry-Lan's unconscious form in the hospital bed. This stranger reminded him of his lost brother, which was unsettling. "Could Mark be somewhere similar, lying safe in a hospital?" he wondered, allowing himself rare hope amidst the uncertainty. The thought was a small comfort, a thin thread reminding him of the brother he missed so profoundly.

Mark was Alex's only sibling and perhaps his only living close relative. Nearly two years prior, Mark had gone missing in action while on manoeuvres in Iraq. The lack of news had been a gnawing pain in Alex's life, a wound refusing to heal. Despite numerous attempts to gather information, the military had provided little, leaving Alex perpetually uncertain. The bond between the two brothers had been strong, especially after their parents passed away. Mark's disappearance had left a void that Alex struggled to fill. Back at home, Mark's wife and son were also left in limbo, not knowing where he was or if he would ever return. Alex's already strained marriage had fallen apart, leading to a divorce. Now, with no children or immediate family to lean on, Mark's absence felt even more profound.

Alex poured himself another drink. Whisky was usually a comfort, but tonight, it was merely a companion to his thoughts. He replayed his conversation with Dr Zayn, the talk of Ry-Lan's mysterious implants, and the unknown script on his uniform. Each piece seemed to drift further away from explanation.

Needing more concrete information, Alex moved from his armchair to his small, cluttered study. He booted up the computer, the screen casting a pale glow in the dimly lit room. Opening a search engine, he typed in descriptions of the symbols and Ry-Lan's unusual uniform, hoping to find anything resembling or explaining what he had seen. He sifted through military databases, articles on advanced technology, and forums discussing experimental medical procedures.

Alex concentrated on articles about Asian data because of the writing on Ry-Lan. He was puzzled about the text, though, as Ry-Lan certainly didn't physically look oriental. If anything, he had more of a Slavic look about him.

His thorough search yielded little more than speculative threads and dead ends. But, despite the lack of immediate results, Alex knew this was only the beginning of a deeper dive into whatever Ry-Lan represented. He jotted down notes on potential avenues for further enquiry, marking researchers to contact and databases to access once he had more specific information.

Finally, fatigue overtook his determination, and Alex slumped back in his chair, rubbing his eyes. The pieces were still scattered, the connections elusive, but his resolve was only strengthened. Tomorrow, he would return to the site, hopeful that new insights might emerge from another sphere examination.

He turned off the computer and went to bed, the day's events casting a long shadow over his thoughts. As sleep finally came, it was fitful, filled with dreams of uniforms and symbols, echoing the unresolved enigma lying just beyond his grasp.

Thu 4th April 2024

The following morning, back on shift, Alex's first stop was the hospital. His concern and curiosity about Ry-Lan's condition drew him back, eager for any new information. Dr Fraser greeted him, now overseeing Ry-Lan's care.

"Sergeant Harper," Dr Fraser shook his hand amicably. "I've heard about your involvement. Ry-Lan, as we're calling him, is under my care now. It's a very challenging situation."

"Any updates on his condition?" Alex asked, his voice reflecting worry and anticipation.

"He's stable but remains unconscious. The implants and unknown compounds in his blood are still puzzling us. We're running more tests to try to understand what we're dealing with. Are you any closer to identifying him?"

Alex wasn't ready to share his limited research with the doctor. "No, nothing yet. But we're on it. We'll let you know when we have something."

As they talked, Alex noticed a subtle movement from Ry-Lan's bed. The man was stirring, his eyes fluttering open. Alex and Dr Fraser moved closer, their expressions registering hope and caution.

Ry-Lan's gaze found Alex, and he seemed to recognise him somehow. Weakly, he tried to speak, but the words came out in a language Alex didn't understand. Despite the language barrier, Ry-Lan's urgency was evident, his eyes pleading with Alex to comprehend. When it was clear that Alex couldn't follow him, Ry-Lan motioned awkwardly towards Alex's phone, indicating that he wanted Alex to film him.

Sensing the importance of the occasion, Alex quickly complied, tilting his phone towards Ry-Lan, who managed to speak a few sentences into the camera. His voice was strained, his effort immense, as if he knew he might not get another chance to communicate his message.

After delivering his message, Ry-Lan looked back at Alex, reaching feebly towards a small Velcro wallet on the bedside table. He gestured for Alex to take it, his insistence clear despite his fading strength. Alex hesitated, but Ry-Lan's persistence was unwavering, so he took the wallet and placed it carefully in his pocket. With that, Ry-Lan's energy seemed to drain, and he fell back into unconsciousness.

Dr Fraser looked over at Alex. "Sergeant, could you wait outside for a moment? I need to attend to him," she requested, her voice calm yet firm. Alex accepted this and stepped out into the hallway.

While waiting, Alex noticed a young Chinese doctor passing and wondered if he was the one who might have identified the name on Ry-Lan's badge. "Excuse me," Alex asked, "were you the doctor who read the name on the man's badge from Bingley farm?"

"Yes. Hi, I'm Doctor Choi," came the confirmation, "can I help you?"

Alex quickly explained and asked, "I recorded a video of him. Would you mind seeing if you can understand what he's saying?"

Dr Choi agreed and watched the video on Alex's phone. After viewing it, he shook his head. "I'm sorry, Sergeant, but I can't make out what he's saying. There are many Chinese dialects, but this doesn't sound like one I am familiar with."

Hope and frustration mounting, Alex suggested, "Are you sure? Would you watch it again and see if you can catch anything at all?"

Dr Choi viewed the video a second time, peering closer. He paused, then said, "I can make out a few words. I think he said 'family,' 'water,' and perhaps 'disease.' It's hard to be sure."

Alex pondered this information. "It seems like he wanted to record a message for someone else. Perhaps his family or his superiors. It's as if he wants it passed on."

Before they could discuss it further, Dr Fraser joined them, expressing sympathy and concern. "He's fighting something, but we're not sure what. Please let me know if you find out anything more about him."

"Yes, of course." Alex was distracted by Ry-Lan's message and the mysterious contents of the wallet now in his possession. He left the hospital, urgency and purpose driving him to uncover what Ry-Lan had been so desperate to communicate.

* * *

After leaving the hospital, Alex examined the wallet in his car. The morning had been emotionally draining, but his mind was buzzing with questions. The wallet was simple, made of a durable, dark fabric, and fastened with Velcro. It felt slightly heavy in his hand, a tangible reminder of the responsibility Ry-Lan had placed on him.

Opening the wallet, Alex found an ID card, but it bore no recognizable institution or familiar insignia. The text, however, was in the same oriental style as the characters on Ry-Lan's uniform. Next, he discovered a small card with intricate writing that seemed like some access card or key. The symbols were foreign to Alex, but he instinctively felt they might be connected to the mysterious machine.

The rest of the wallet contained a few personal items, such as a family photograph and a handful of odd-looking coins or tokens. The photograph showed a small group of people smiling warmly at the camera. Alex studied their faces, wondering if they were Ry-Lan's family or his colleagues.

The coins were unusual, not resembling any familiar currency. They were round and unusually made of plastic, with similar characters etched into their surfaces as those on the access card. The realisation that these coins might be from somewhere beyond his known world sent a shiver down Alex's spine. The possibility that Ry-Lan could be a traveller from somewhere out of this world seemed both thrilling and daunting.

Putting the wallet back in his pocket, Alex felt a surge of determination. He needed to understand what Ry-Lan was trying to convey and what the mysterious writing represented. The wallet was a clue, possibly the key to unlocking the sphere's secrets.

With the wallet safely tucked away, Alex thought about his next move. The photograph, the ID, the coins, the access card—all were pieces of a puzzle that demanded solving. He would start by comparing the symbols on the card with those on the sphere, hoping they might align and unlock more answers.

As Alex drove away from the hospital, he set his mind on the challenges ahead. Determined to follow the trail to its end, he knew the journey would be challenging, but he resolved to uncover the truth, no matter where it led.

*　*　*

Alex drove towards the farm, his thoughts filled with anticipation and curiosity. The sun now sat higher in the sky, casting shadows across the Yorkshire Moors. Alex's focus was sharp, yet his mind wandered to the video he had recorded of Ry-Lan's halting message. The memory of Ry-Lan's urgency replayed in his mind, leaving him wondering what secrets it held.

As he navigated the familiar rural roads, Alex's thoughts drifted to Ry-Lan himself. Who was he? Where did he come from? The more Alex pondered these questions, the more he felt an invisible current of mystery swirling around him. There was something otherworldly about Ry-Lan, something that suggested his origins lay beyond the ordinary.

The farm came into view, and Alex's determination heightened. The sphere and Ry-Lan were pieces of a puzzle he was set on solving, no matter how complex or daunting it seemed. The anticipation of uncovering new clues and the thrill of exploring the unknown drove him forward, eager to continue the investigation.

Alex approached Bingley farm with a sense of anticipation. He couldn't shake the feeling that today would bring new revelations, possibly answers to questions swirling in his mind since Ry-Lan's arrival. What secrets did the sphere hold? What message was Ry-Lan trying to convey? The possibilities loomed large as Alex prepared to move into the unknown again.

Chapter 3

Tommy was waiting by the gate as Alex pulled up. The farmer's face was etched with unease, his eyes scanning the horizon as if expecting something else extraordinary to appear. "It's still here," Tommy said as Alex climbed out of his police car. "And I ain't touched it, just as you asked."

"Good," Alex replied, reassuringly smiling at the farmer. "I appreciate you keeping it secure."

With an understanding gesture, Tommy pointed towards the field where the machine lay. "Take all the time you need, Alex. I'll give you some space."

As Alex trekked across the field, the machine came into view, gleaming in the bright sunlight. The air was still, amplifying the low hum emanating from the sphere. With its polished surface reflecting the surroundings like a distorted mirror, the machine looked both alien and oddly beautiful.

Alex approached it cautiously, the unease of the previous day replaced with a focused determination. The sphere stood as an enigma, a silent guardian of secrets yet to be revealed. He could almost feel a burden of curiosity pressing on him, urging him forward.

Standing before the machine, Alex glanced around the quiet field, the only other sounds coming from the distant bleating of sheep and the occasional chirping of birds. The solitude of the scene contrasted sharply with the complexity of the task ahead. Taking a deep breath, Alex reached into his pocket and pulled out the card he had retrieved from Ry-Lan's wallet. The figures on the card glinted faintly in the sunlight, hinting at their potential importance.

With renewed resolve, Alex moved closer to the machine, ready to uncover its secrets. Tense anticipation filled the air as he prepared to use the card, his thoughts whirling about what he might find inside.

Holding up the card, Alex examined it closely, comparing its symbols to those on the machine's panel. The symbols matched, and with cautious anticipation, Alex placed the card against the panel. Immediately, a faint beep sounded, and a hatch slid open, revealing an opening large enough for a person to climb through easily.

Peering inside, Alex saw a dimly lit interior, illuminated only by the soft glow of control panels and screens. The air inside was crisp and clean, like freshly sanitised equipment, with a faint hint of antiseptic. He hesitated momentarily, his hand hovering over the edge of the hatch. The machine's interior beckoned him, a promise of answers to the mystery governing his thoughts.

Breathing deeply, Alex climbed through the hatch and entered the sphere. The interior confounded him, the smooth, metallic walls curving around his body in a seamless dome. The lighting came from hidden sources, casting a soft, ambient glow highlighting sleek surfaces.

In front of him, a single chair sat before a complex control console filled with buttons, switches, and touchscreens. The screens displayed a series of unfamiliar characters, similar to those on Ry-Lan's badge and the card Alex held. The chair, though futuristic in appearance, looked inviting, as if designed for comfort during extended use.

Looking around, Alex noticed several other panels lining the walls, each adorned with glowing buttons and displays. The atmosphere inside the machine was quiet, with only the faintest hum coming from the equipment. The temperature was comfortably cool, adding to the surreal feeling of being inside an advanced piece of technology.

As Alex explored the interior, mixed emotions washed over him—fear, curiosity, awe. He marvelled at the sleek design and advanced technology, contemplating the machine's purpose and origins. The layout was unlike anything he had seen, yet it felt strangely intuitive as if designed for human use.

Alex's heart raced as he sat in the chair inside the machine. The seat felt really comfortable, cushioned, and contoured to fit the human body perfectly. The control console spread out before him, gleaming with an array of equipment, all marked with the same type of strange text.

The machine's interior resembled a science fiction movie. The walls consisted of a sleek, metallic material, smooth to the touch, made all the more beautiful by the ambient light. The controls were backlit, illuminating the foreign characters etched into them. Alex's gaze travelled across the various screens, noting the intricacy of the information displayed.

Awe and apprehension initially ruled Alex's emotions. The advanced technology before him was inconceivable, yet there was a strange familiarity with how the controls were arranged. His mind swirled as he tried to understand what he saw, and curiosity outweighed his fear.

As he surveyed the controls, Alex's hands hovered over the touchscreens and buttons, his fingers tingling with expectancy. The symbols on the displays were similar to those on Ry-Lan's badge, hinting at a connection between man and machine. Alex felt consumed by responsibility as he prepared to interact with the controls, knowing that the machine might hold the key to understanding Ry-Lan's message.

The machine's layout was intuitive, with the control chair positioned centrally in front of the main console. The touchscreens were responsive, and the buttons clicked softly under Alex's fingers. The ambient lighting and gentle hum of the equipment created an atmosphere both calming and unsettling.

Alex's curiosity grew as he examined the various controls. He pulled out his phone and tried using a translation app to decipher the text on the displays. However, he quickly realised he had no signal inside the machine's metallic structure, making the app non-functional. The lack of a signal brought an unexpected obstacle, but Alex was undeterred.

Determined to understand the writing, Alex exited the machine and waited outside momentarily, raising his phone to get a signal. After a few minutes, the phone buzzed to life, and he quickly downloaded the offline Chinese dictionary for translation. Armed with this new tool, Alex was ready to try again.

Re-entering the machine, Alex focused on the task at hand. He loaded the translation app and switched to camera mode, using the offline dictionary to tackle the mysterious characters. Inside the machine, the lighting remained unchanged, providing a peaceful environment for Alex to work. The buzz of the equipment seemed to fade into the background as he concentrated on decoding the controls.

With the offline dictionary ready, Alex pointed his phone at the writing on the displays and began translating. The translations were not perfect, often providing vague or confusing results. With patience and persistence, Alex managed to decipher a few key terms hinting at the machine's functionality. The process was slow and required careful attention, but Alex felt more accomplished with each successful translation.

Continuing to work, Alex realised that the characters were part of a sophisticated language, possibly a derivative of Chinese or another similar script. The language barrier added to the challenge, but Alex's resolve pushed him forward. He focused on key terms and phrases, hoping to uncover clues explaining the machine's purpose.

Despite the initial challenges, Alex grew confident in navigating the machine's controls. The offline dictionary provided just enough information to give him a starting point, and his methodical approach allowed him to make slow but steady progress. The experience was a combination of trial and error, with each step bringing him closer to understanding the machine's secrets.

Despite his careful approach, Alex's interactions inadvertently triggered a command, and the hatch suddenly slid shut behind him with a soft hiss. Panic surged as he leapt up and tried to open the door manually. The edges of the hatch were perfectly sealed, leaving no visible gap. He quickly realised that brute force wouldn't help.

Alex returned to the control chair, instead deciding to try to open the door using the controls. He examined the touchscreens, hoping to find a command to reopen the door. As he looked through the translations, one of the words stood out. The word translated using his phone as "to allow." Seizing this clue, he pressed the button, hoping it would unlock the hatch.

Immediately, a new screen appeared, displaying information with two options beneath it. The translation tool detected the word "confirm" among the text, above what Alex deduced to be "yes" and "no" choices. Feeling more confident, Alex pressed what he believed to be the "yes" button.

The machine responded instantly, coming to life with a hum that filled the interior. Bright lights illuminated the space, casting sharp shadows across the sleek, metallic surfaces. The unexpected response startled Alex, and the screens around him seemed to change mode. On the main screen, the number "30" appeared prominently.

At first, Alex felt relief at seeing a familiar symbol. However, he soon realised that the numbers were counting down, indicating something else was happening. The hum grew louder, resonating through the control chair, and the bright lights and sounds filled the enclosed space, creating urgency and tension.

The timer continued ticking down on the main screen, the numbers changing steadily. Alex's heart beat faster as he stared at the countdown, his initial relief giving way to a sense of impending doom. The machine vibrated slightly, and the hum grew louder, signalling that something significant was about to happen.

Alex's first instinct was to try to stop the countdown. He frantically pressed buttons and swiped at the touchscreens, hoping to reverse the process. Each interaction only seemed to solidify the machine's commitment to its course. The countdown moved forward, and Alex's attempts to halt it proved futile.

As the seconds ticked away, Alex's initial panic transformed into an enforced calm. He realised he couldn't prevent whatever the machine had planned and began mentally preparing for the unknown. His breaths came in shallow gasps, and his pulse pounded in his ears.

The machine's vibrations grew more intense, and the lights brightened, creating an atmosphere of anticipation. Alex's mind raced as he considered what might be happening but found no answers. The ancillary screens displayed a flurry of data, and the countdown neared its end.

Chapter 4

The display in front of Alex flickered and then steadied. His stomach churned as the vibrations intensified, the whole machine seeming to pulse with energy. For a moment, he felt the weight of his body lessen, as if gravity itself was loosening its grip on him.

A brilliant light enveloped him, so intense that he had to close his eyes against the glare. The sensations that followed were disorienting—his body felt as though it was being stretched and compressed simultaneously. It was a sensory overload, unlike anything Alex had ever experienced. The noise, the light, the feeling of motionless movement—pushing the limits of his endurance was overwhelming.

And then quickly, the intensity of the light and vibrations diminished. The machine's hum receded to a whisper, and the bright lights dimmed to a gentle glow. Alex opened his eyes slowly, his body still tingling from the journey. He was unsure of what he would find when he looked outside the machine—if the world as he knew it had changed in ways beyond comprehension.

Alex thought, trying to carefully remember the sequence of commands that had inadvertently sealed the hatch, and he again scrutinised the touchscreen intently. His previous misstep was a lesson in caution, and he was determined not to repeat it. His fingers hovered over the screen, tracing the word he had realised meant "close." In its place, he saw a new symbol that his offline translator suggested could mean "open." With hope and trepidation, Alex pressed the symbol, half-expecting another unexpected response from the machine.

To his relief, the command was correct this time. The hatch responded immediately, the locking mechanism disengaging with a soft click before the door slid open with a quiet hiss. He stepped out, his legs unsteady from the physical disorientation and the mental strain of navigating the unknown. As his boots touched the ground, he blinked against the brightness of the sun—a sun that cast shadows slightly askew from how he remembered them just moments before. The subtle difference in the scenery alerted his suspicions: Had he travelled? Why did things look similar, but not the same? The suspicion brought cautious optimism, mingling with a profound awareness of his new reality.

Wed 3rd April 2024

As his eyes adjusted to the subtle differences in the light, Alex cautiously stepped forward, scanning the environment. The farm was unmistakably the same place he had left moments ago, but the air carried a crispness that hinted at a time not his own. Details were slightly off: the shadows were longer, the colours of the moorland flora were more profound, and the silence draped a denser blanket over the terrain.

Alex's thoughts buzzed as he tried to piece together the clues. Now quiet behind him, the machine seemed like a relic already integrating into this slightly altered world. He turned to observe it, half-expecting it to vanish, leaving him stranded in this unfamiliar version of familiar grounds.

As Alex's eyes adjusted to the light and his surroundings, he quickly noticed another machine on the field. His gaze first fell on the original machine beside which he had initially discovered Ry-Lan. It sat ominously a short distance away, its surface reflecting the morning sun with a gleam that seemed simultaneously familiar and foreign. A figure, unmistakably Ry-Lan, emerged from this other machine, his movements unsteady and cautious as if every step was a monumental effort. Alex watched, his heart pounding, as Ry-Lan staggered, leaning on the machine for support.

Turning his attention back to his immediate vicinity, Alex realised with a start that the machine he had just exited was positioned slightly differently than where he had activated it. The grass underneath it was undisturbed, suggesting it hadn't crashed but materialised seamlessly in this new location. This subtle displacement was a silent testament to the machine's capabilities, reinforcing the reality of his temporal journey. The implications of this realisation sent a shiver down his spine, intertwining awe with a deepening sense of the complexities he now faced in the woven tapestry of time.

Alex turned back to watch Ry-Lan collapse to his knees, overwhelmed or exhausted by his journey. This scene mirrored the past, a living replay of what must have happened after Ry-Lan first arrived. The realisation of witnessing the events immediately following Ry-Lan's arrival anchored Alex's swirling thoughts: had he travelled back to the very day Ry-Lan had appeared on the Yorkshire Moors?

With a heightened awareness of responsibility, Alex hurried towards Ry-Lan, retracing the steps he knew led to the man in need. As he approached, the details of Ry-Lan's condition became clearer—the same disorientation and laboured breathing he had seen before. Yet now, knowing what he did, each observation carried the knowledge of their shared displacement in time.

Alex reached Ry-Lan, barely conscious and murmuring incoherently in the same cryptic language as he had spoken before. Kneeling beside him, Alex felt the echo of their first encounter, a surreal doubling of moments across time. He reached out, trying to offer comfort or aid, but Ry-Lan's eyes barely flickered in recognition. The man was lost in his own ordeal, as unreachable now as he had been in the future.

* * *

As Alex tried to stabilise Ry-Lan, a faint noise from the opposite direction caught his attention. He lifted his gaze and froze, his breath catching in his throat. Not far from where he knelt, another figure stood—a man who bore an uncanny resemblance to himself. This other "Alex" was stationed near a third machine, its presence as incongruous as the first, angled away behind his own machine.

This doppelganger was not just passively observing but was actively recording the scene with a phone. The surreal realisation of looking at himself, separated by mere moments or dimensions, sent a shiver down Alex's spine. The other Alex seemed just as perplexed, his actions cautious and deliberate as he captured every detail of the scene unfolding.

Driven by a profound sense of responsibility, Alex hesitated only momentarily, watching the figure that mirrored his every feature. He felt a fleeting connection to this other Alex, a surreal acknowledgement of their shared, bizarre circumstance. But a cry from Ry-Lan forced Alex to turn his attention back to the immediate urgency. As he shifted his focus, the other Alex and the third machine faded from his consciousness. Alex's resolve hardened as he tried to help Ry-Lan, who seemed increasingly unstable with each laboured breath. Despite the language barrier and Ry-Lan's weakened state, Alex attempted to communicate, offering words of reassurance that felt hollow in the vastness of their shared displacement.

Ry-Lan's eyes met his briefly, a glimmer of recognition—or perhaps gratitude—in his gaze before slipping back into a fitful half-consciousness. The pressure of what had happened and the overlapping realities or timelines bore down on Alex, making him acutely aware of the fragility and complexity of their circumstances.

Alex steadied himself beside the now silent Ry-Lan, his mind ablaze with the implications of what he had just witnessed. The presence of multiple instances of himself interacting with the timeline almost independently solidified his suspicion: he was not just traversing back and forth in time but potentially across overlapping timelines.

The quietness of the farm was punctuated only by the distant sound of the machines, a reminder of the technological marvel that had brought him to this moment. Each breath Alex took felt laden with the burden of his newfound understanding. The environment, so familiar yet altered by the events he had witnessed, seemed to echo his turmoil.

* * *

Determined to gain control of the events and perhaps to return to his original timeline—or at least to a version where he could make sense of these anomalies—Alex returned to his machine. His steps were measured, each one taken with a deep awareness of the extraordinary circumstances he was navigating.

Upon reaching the machine, Alex paused, with the card in his hand hovering over the panel he had previously activated. His previous fear had transformed into a resolute need to understand and perhaps control the machine's capabilities. He recalled the sequences he had inadvertently initiated and considered the possible outcomes of another jump.

He decided with a mixture of caution and desperation. He needed answers, and the only way to seek them was to engage further with the machine's mysterious technology. With a deep breath, he initiated the sequence for another jump, his mind focused on the potential repercussions. He was aware this could spiral further into chaos or lead him closer to unravelling the time-bending puzzle.

As the machine began to hum, signalling the start of another temporal transition, Alex braced himself. He reviewed everything he had observed and learned so far, trying to predict where or when he might end up this time. The digital display flickered to life, the familiar countdown beginning anew.

With each passing second, the intensity of the situation grew. Alex's thoughts turned inward, questioning the nature of reality and his place within these unfolding mysteries. As the machine vibrated under the increasing power of its operation, he prepared for the unknown, ready to face whatever time—or times—might reveal next.

As the machine's hum subsided and the bright light enveloping Alex dimmed, he cautiously stepped out with his senses alert to any new changes. The scene of the farm greeted him once more, but subtle differences in the positioning of nearby objects and the sun's angle suggested that he had returned to the same timeline again.

* * *

Alex climbed out of the machine and was confronted by the other two machines. He watched in stunned silence as another version of himself emerged from the nearest machine, about ten metres away. The surreal sight of his own figure stepping out into the daylight was disorienting, amplifying the strangeness of the entire ordeal.

Not far from where this other Alex appeared, Ry-Lan was near the original machine from which he had first been discovered. Ry-Lan's movements were laboured and unsteady; his form slumped against the side of the sphere as if seeking support from its solid structure.

Compelled to document this bizarre experience, Alex pulled out his phone. He began filming the scene, capturing the eerie stillness punctuated only by the soft mechanical whirring of the machines. His camera panned over the area, recording the juxtaposition of familiar farm elements with the incongruous technology intruding into this rural setting.

As he continued to film, the other Alex moved towards Ry-Lan, who lay still near the original machine. The footage captured his approach, showing his careful examination of Ry-Lan, who appeared just as he had left him—unconscious but alive. This other Alex then looked at him, and he felt a strange déjà vu of this event that had happened just minutes ago.

The machine's gentle hum faded into the background as Alex stood motionless, phone in hand, recording his own disoriented movements from moments before. The sight of himself on the small screen—his past self rushing to aid Ry-Lan—was unnerving, yet it solidified his understanding of the complex temporal web that entangled him. Each action he witnessed reminded him of his choices and the inexplicable reality he now faced.

Alex then stopped the recording and put down his phone, his thoughts full of the data he had just collected. The visual record was not just for his report; it was a beacon of sanity in the chaos, a way to anchor his experiences to something tangible.

His recording captured the surreal tableau: two versions of himself and multiple iterations of the same event playing out from a different perspective each time. The quiet of the morning, punctuated only by the occasional mechanical whir from the machines, added to the otherworldly atmosphere.

As he stood there, the magnitude of his situation pressed down upon him. The farm, a place of life and growth, now held a dual role as the stage for a profound cosmic puzzle. Alex knew the answers he sought were tied not just to the machine or Ry-Lan but to the very fabric of reality itself. A web of temporal anomalies ensnared him, each jump through time revealing more layers and leaving more questions.

Determined yet daunted, Alex prepared to engage with the machines once again. He knew his journey through time was far from over, and each step brought new revelations and challenges. Resolve and unease filled him as he looked at the silent, humming machines. The path forward was uncertain, but Alex Harper was not one to shy away from the unknown.

Alex's thoughts raced overtime. The realisation that he was not just crossing into different times but potentially creating overlapping realities was overwhelming. The implications were vast and unsettling. How many timelines had his actions influenced? What were the consequences of his presence in these repeated moments?

Standing beside the humming machine, seeming to pulse with an energy of its own, Alex felt a profound sense of isolation. The moors around him were quiet as if holding their breath at the unfolding drama. He was far from home in more ways than one, disconnected from his time and any familiar reality.

With the significance of his discoveries bearing down on him, Alex tried to think what he should do. The silence that followed was heavy, filled with the echoes of his uncovered truths. He was alone with his thoughts, the vast Yorkshire Moors expending no comfort, only a harsh reminder of his solitude.

"How can I get home?" he thought. The machine beside him gently hummed, its presence a constant reminder of the unknown forces at play.

As he stood there, contemplating his next move, the machine emitted a soft beep, a signal that it was ready for another journey. Alex's heart skipped a beat. Was he ready to face what came next? Could he ever return to the life he knew before?

Chapter 5

Alex stepped back inside the machine, filled with trepidation yet determined. He settled into the control chair, the familiar cool scent of the machine filling his senses. The screens glowed softly, displaying the same cryptic writing he had puzzled over since his first encounter with the device.

Alex knew he had to find a way to return to his original timeline. The burden of his plight grew steadily, but he forced himself to stay calm and methodical. He pulled out his phone and opened the offline translation app, ready to decode the characters once more.

He scanned the screens, focusing on translating each symbol carefully. Alex realised he had been telling the machine to repeat its previous action, leading to the repeated time shifts. This time, he needed to find a command to return him to a previous origin point instead.

The process was slow and meticulous. Alex's fingers trembled slightly as he traced each symbol, cross-referencing them with the translations on his phone. He found a set of characters that seemed to correspond with the concept of "point of origin," but he needed certainty. He rechecked his work multiple times, knowing that a single mistake could lead to further disorientation or danger.

As Alex continued to double-check his translations, a growing worry gnawed at him. What if he had missed something critical? The implications of an error were too severe to ignore. He decided he needed to verify his findings and get more information. With this in mind, he exited the machine again and walked away, holding his phone up for a signal.

He wandered around the field, his eyes glued to the screen, hoping for even a single reception bar. The frustration mounted as Alex came to terms with his lack of success. He reluctantly returned to the machine, accepting that his only choice was to rely on his own translations and instincts.

Hours passed as he painstakingly deciphered the instructions. Despite the cool atmosphere inside the machine, sweat beaded on Alex's forehead, and his eyes ached from the strain of focusing on the small, intricate characters. The seriousness of the situation was apparent to him. Every moment spent inside the machine felt like a gamble, but he knew he had no option but to press on.

Finally, after what felt like an eternity, Alex felt confident enough to navigate the menus and screens of the machine's interface. It wasn't just about pressing the right button—but about understanding the layers of menus and submenus to find the machine's point of origin history. Each screen he accessed brought him closer to the information he needed, but it was a painstaking process of trial and error.

Taking a deep breath, Alex delved deeper into the interface, carefully interpreting the words and piecing together the machine's navigational history. The machine responded with a series of beeps and flashes, acknowledging each command. The tension in the air was palpable as he finally found a screen displaying a list of origins. His heart pounded as he selected the origin point from "two jumps" ago, hoping it would take him back to his original timeline. He was patient, and it took a while to translate and be confident enough to use the machine again.

The machine whirred to life, the soft hum growing into a resonant vibration that Alex could feel deep in his bones. The now-familiar sensation of time travel enveloped him—weightlessness, brief disorientation, and then blinding light that seemed to pierce through the fabric of reality itself. This time, the experience felt slightly more controlled, as if the machine guided him more gently through the temporal shift.

Thu 4th April 2024

As the vibrations subsided and the light dimmed, Alex opened the hatch and saw he was back at the farm. He blinked against the early morning sunlight streaming through the hatch, which had opened seamlessly at the journey's end. He stepped out cautiously, his legs steady but his head full of questions.

The farm was eerily quiet, bathed in the morning's soft, golden light. The scene was almost exactly as he remembered it before his travels began. The moors' tranquillity stood in clear contrast to the turmoil he had just experienced. The sheep grazed peacefully in the distance, oblivious to the extraordinary events.

Alex took a deep breath, the crisp morning air filling his lungs and grounding him. He glanced around, noting the familiar landmarks and the unchanged terrain. Everything appeared just as it had been as if no time had passed.

Pulling out his phone, Alex checked for a signal. He had two bars. Alex also noticed the time matched his original departure, confirming that he had returned to his original timeline. A wave of relief washed over him, but the burden of his experiences tempered it. The knowledge he had gained, the mysteries he had encountered, and the machine's potential implications all added to the load on his mind.

Standing in the quiet morning light, Alex felt overwhelming relief and gratitude. Dropping to his knees, he pressed his lips to the cold, dewy grass, tasting the earth and feeling the solid ground beneath him. The raw, familiar texture grounded him, anchoring him in the reality to which he had fought so hard to return. Emotions engulfed him, a combination of triumph and exhaustion but also a burgeoning resolve. He knew his journey was far from over. The mysteries he had encountered, and the machine's connotations threatened to overload his mind. As he rose, wiping away tears, he felt a deep-seated determination to understand the true nature of the machine and the reality-bending experiences he had endured.

Alex breathed deeply, trying to steady his racing heart. The relief of being back was quickly overshadowed by the realisation of the mysteries and potential dangers the machine posed. He knew he was in over his head. The implications of what he had witnessed and experienced went far beyond his training as a police sergeant.

As he stood there, his mind accelerated through the possibilities. What should he tell the chief inspector? She had requested an update but had left the matter in his hands. CI West had also seemed unusually downbeat and, Alex supposed, in no mood for talk of a time machine. He paused, and as he thought about the peril he had been in, a sense of anger and resentment bubbled up. His profession had always been about protecting others, but now he had felt exposed and vulnerable.

No, he decided; he resented the idea of trusting in the bureaucratic process. He needed someone who could understand the science behind the machine and help him make sense of the impossible. And he knew exactly who to call.

Brian Mitchell was an old friend from his university days, a brilliant physicist now teaching at Durham University. Scrolling through his phone, Alex quickly found Brian's number, his fingers trembling slightly as he pressed the call button.

The phone rang a few times before Brian answered. "Hello, Alex? It's been a while!"

"Brian, it's good to hear your voice," Alex said, his tone more urgent than he'd intended. "I need your help. I've stumbled upon something ... extraordinary. You're not going to believe it, but I think it involves time manipulation."

After a brief silence, Brian replied, his voice cautious but intrigued. "Time manipulation? Alex, what exactly are you talking about?"

"It's a long story, but I don't think I can explain it over the phone. Can we meet? I need you to see this for yourself."

Brian hesitated for a moment. "Alright, come to the university. I'll clear my schedule for this afternoon. This sounds too intriguing to pass up."

"Thanks, Brian. I'll be there as soon as I can." Alex hung up the phone, feeling a modicum of relief. Brian's expertise was exactly what he needed to understand the machine and the bizarre events he had experienced.

As he drove towards Durham, his mind was a whirlwind of thoughts. The questions about the machine, Ry-Lan, and the overlapping timelines consumed him. He replayed the events, trying to piece together the puzzle fragments. His anger towards his profession was still there, simmering beneath the surface, but a sense of determination now accompanied it.

He had taken the first step in seeking help, and with Brian's knowledge, he hoped to uncover the truth behind the mysterious machine and the phenomena it had unleashed. The journey ahead was uncertain, but Alex knew he wouldn't face it alone.

* * *

Alex arrived at Durham University just after midday, his heart pounding with anticipation and anxiety. As he walked through the familiar campus, memories of his younger days at the university flooded back. Brian had arranged to meet him in his office, a cluttered but cosy room filled with books, papers, and scientific equipment. The familiar smell of old books and coffee brought a sense of nostalgia, briefly grounding Alex in the normalcy of their friendship.

"Alex, come in," Brian greeted warmly as Alex entered. But Alex was taken aback by the sight of his old friend. Brian looked significantly older than he remembered, with deeper lines etched into his face and more grey in his hair. The years had clearly been demanding on him. "You sounded pretty urgent on the phone. What's going on?"

Alex took a deep breath, trying to gather his thoughts. He knew he had to explain the situation without sounding like he had lost his grip on reality. "Brian, this is going to sound crazy, but I need you to keep an open mind." He paused, searching for the right words. "I found a machine. A strange, spherical machine. And ... I think it can manipulate time."

Brian raised an eyebrow, clearly sceptical but willing to listen. "Manipulate time? That's a bold claim, Alex. You'd better have some solid evidence."

"I do," Alex said, pulling out his phone. "I recorded video footage of the events. And I've tried to piece together what I understand about the machine's functions." He handed the phone to Brian and played the video.

As Brian watched, his expression shifted from scepticism to intrigue. The footage showed the other instances of Alex and the bizarre overlapping timelines. Alex narrated the events, explaining how he had interacted with the machine and the strange occurrences that followed. Watching the video again, Alex bubbled with emotion. Seeing himself interact with the machine and the surreal events unfold brought a lump to his throat. It was all so overpowering, and he again realised the seriousness of what had happened.

Brian tapped his fingers thoughtfully on the armrest of his chair. "This is ... extraordinary. If what you're showing me is real, it could challenge our fundamental understanding of time and physics." He looked at Alex, his eyes sharp with intellectual curiosity. "But I want to see this machine for myself. It's one thing to watch a video; it's another to examine the actual device."

"I understand," Alex replied. "I was hoping you'd say that. There's so much we don't know, and I want your expertise to make sense of it."

Brian agreed, still cautious but clearly fascinated. "Alright, I'll come to see it with you. We need to approach this scientifically, with careful observation and documentation. If this machine is what we think it is, we must be thorough."

As they began discussing the logistics of their visit to the farm, Brian's initial scepticism gave way to a growing excitement tempered by a deep foreboding. He mused aloud about the machine's origins, his voice hinting unease. "Could it be some secret project from China? Or ... from the future? The technology you're describing is surely too advanced to be current."

Alex shrugged, his mind full of possibilities, each more daunting than the last. "I honestly don't know. But every clue we've got suggests it's beyond anything we currently understand. And that's what scares me."

The potential implications of their findings were immense, and both men felt the strain of responsibility. The idea that the machine could either be a product of a major superpower or a visitor from the future was deeply unsettling.

* * *

After a long and intense discussion, Brian sat back in his chair, his expression thoughtful. "I've been thinking, Alex," he began slowly, "what if this machine isn't just manipulating time but also creating or accessing parallel realities? What if your actions have already altered more than we can perceive?"

Alex stared at him, the substance of Brian's words sinking in. "Parallel realities? You mean, there could be more versions of me out there, all experiencing different outcomes?"

"Exactly. It's a complex theory, but it would explain why you saw multiple instances of yourself and Ry-Lan. Each jump you make might not just move you through time but also into a different reality altogether."

The implications were staggering. Alex's mind buzzed as he considered that every action he took could have far-reaching consequences, not just in his own timeline but in countless others. The enormity of their discovery was mind-boggling, and for a moment, the room felt oppressively small.

Brian leaned forward, his eyes intense. "We need to approach this scientifically. Gather data, run controlled experiments, and understand the machine's full capabilities and limitations. We need to be careful and methodical. We cannot afford any mistakes."

Motivated by Brian's theory and the need for concrete answers, they quickly formulated a plan. They would visit the machine together the next morning to conduct more controlled experiments and gather more data. Brian insisted on bringing scientific equipment and tools, adding a layer of realism and preparation to their next steps.

"I'll need to go home and pick up some gear," Brian said, already making a mental checklist. "Sensors, recording devices, maybe even some basic lab equipment. We need to document everything meticulously."

Alex agreed, appreciating Brian's thoroughness. They arranged to meet at the farm at dawn, determined to face the unknown with a blend of scientific rigour and cautious optimism. As they parted ways, Alex felt a renewed sense of purpose, tempered by the sobering realisation of the complexities they were about to explore.

Chapter 6

Brian sat in his home study, the soft glow of the desk lamp casting a warm light over his desk. Usually tidy, it was now cluttered with papers and open books. He had been researching relevant scientific principles and potential technologies ever since his conversation with Alex. He felt a frisson of excitement in anticipation of seeing the mysterious machine Alex had described.

He could hear the muffled sounds of his wife, Emily, and their son, Danny, in the kitchen. Pushing his chair back, Brian decided to join them. As he entered the kitchen, he saw Danny at the table, eating supper and chatting animatedly about his day at school.

Emily looked up and smiled. "Hey, you've been in your cave all evening, you know," she teased gently.

Brian chuckled. "Just needed a break. It's been a long day."

Emily set down a pot of tea and poured a cup for Brian. "So, what's this big discovery you're off to investigate tomorrow? You seemed pretty excited earlier."

Brian sipped his tea, considering his words carefully. He didn't want to alarm her with talk of time machines and unknown dangers. "An old friend from university, Alex, found something unusual near Helmworth. He's asking for my help to figure out what it is. It's probably nothing, but it could be an interesting scientific find."

Emily sensed more to the story but knew better than to press. "Well, just be careful, okay? I don't want you getting into anything dangerous."

"I will," Brian assured her. "It likely won't amount to anything, but it will be nice to get out into the countryside for a change."

After supper, Brian returned to his study to check over his equipment: an EMF meter, a Geiger counter, an infrared thermometer, a laptop, a video camera, a radio signal detector, and a tool kit.

He carefully gathered the items, packing them into a sturdy backpack along with a thick woollen sweater. As he worked, he considered the possibilities. What if this machine really did manipulate time? The implications were staggering.

Stepping back into the hall, Brian took a moment to look at his family. He saw Emily reading on the couch and Danny finishing up his homework, a frown on his forehead. Brian sighed; the world had become such a complex place, filled with uncertainties and challenges. He hoped that whatever he discovered tomorrow would be something he could share with them, something that would make sense of the chaos.

Later, as Emily and Danny went to bed, Brian lingered in his study, reflecting on the day's events. He looked down at the lock screen photo on his computer—a picture of Emily and Danny smiling on a family holiday. Danny didn't smile half as much as he used to, and it bothered Brian because whatever it was, Danny wasn't letting on. Nonetheless, the photo gave him a moment of solace amidst the whirlwind of thoughts about the upcoming investigation.

Lying in bed that night, Brian's thoughts kept returning to the machine. Despite the risks, the scientist in him couldn't help but feel a thrill at the thought of what he might discover. He drifted off to sleep, his dreams filled with images of advanced technology and the promise of uncovering something truly extraordinary.

Fri 5th April 2024

The next morning, Brian set off early for Bingley farm, his backpack loaded with carefully selected equipment. The journey from his home to the countryside felt like a trip to another world. As he drove, the cityscape gradually gave way to rolling hills and vast, open fields. The transition from concrete to greenery was striking, and while it held a certain charm, Brian couldn't help but feel slightly out of place.

As Brian navigated the winding country roads, he became stuck behind a flock of sheep being herded across the road, a situation unimaginable in the city. The journey to the farm tested his patience and adaptability, with his car struggling on the uneven terrain of muddy tracks and damp ground. When he finally arrived, the unusual smells and sounds of the countryside hit him, heightening his sense of unease.

He saw Alex waiting for him near the entrance as he approached. Seeing a familiar figure against this unfamiliar backdrop felt like a blessing.

"Morning, Brian!" Alex called out, waving as Brian brought his car to a stop. "How was the drive?"

"Eventful," Brian replied with a grin, stepping out of the car and stretching his legs. "I'm not exactly used to the countryside. It's ... different."

Alex chuckled, patting Brian on the shoulder. "You'll be fine. Come on; let me introduce you to Tommy."

"Tommy" Thompson, the farmer who owned the land, was waiting by the gate, leaning casually on it while chewing a piece of straw. He eyed Brian with curiosity and wariness, quickly sensing that Brian was not entirely comfortable with the locale.

"Tommy, this is Brian Mitchell, the physicist I told you about," Alex said, making the introductions. "Brian, this is Tommy. He's been kind enough to let us probe the machine on his property."

"Nice to meet you, Tommy," Brian said, extending his hand.

Tommy shook it firmly. "Morning, Brian. Hope you can make some sense of that thing out there. It's been a real head-scratcher."

Tommy noticed Brian's city shoes and the mud already clinging to them. "Sorry about the mess. If you need, I've got some boots you can borrow," he offered.

Brian glanced down at his shoes, then back at Tommy, appreciating the gesture but declining politely. "Thanks, Tommy, but I'll manage."

With the formalities out of the way, Alex led Brian across the field to where the machine lay. The ground was damp and slightly muddy, making Brian wish he'd taken up Tommy's offer of boots. The machine was just as Alex had described—gleaming and otherworldly, its polished surface reflecting the morning light. The high-tech marvel stood out against the rustic setting, underscoring the divide between advanced technology and the simple, earthy environment.

Brian set down his backpack and began unpacking his equipment. He felt excitement and anticipation building as he prepared to examine the machine up close. His first impression was one of awe at the sophisticated design and the materials, which seemed far beyond contemporary technology.

He started with an initial sweep of the machine's exterior, using the EMF meter to measure any electromagnetic fields. The readings were high but consistent, indicating the machine was active but stable. Next, he used the Geiger counter to check for radiation and was relieved to find none.

"I've never seen anything like this," Brian muttered, more to himself than anyone else, as he continued his examination. He switched on the video camera, documenting every detail, and took out the infrared thermometer to measure the machine's surface temperature. The readings were again normal, much to his relief.

As he worked, Brian narrated his observations into the camera, describing the machine's exterior and interior. The smooth, metallic surface, the seamless joints, and the intricate writing—all of it was fascinating and perplexing.

Alex watched with interest, occasionally pointing out features and explaining how he'd used the translation app to understand some of the words. Brian took notes in his notepad detailing his observations.

After thoroughly examining the exterior, Brian moved to the interior, carefully stepping into the machine. He used the radio signal detector to scan for transmissions, noting that the machine blocked radio signals from outside. Every step was methodical, aimed at uncovering the machine's secrets.

As the morning progressed, Alex explained what he had already observed, sharing his insights with Brian. The farm's tranquillity sharply juxtaposed the intensity of their investigation, each discovery bringing them closer to understanding the machine's purpose and origins.

Brian felt a renewed sense of camaraderie with Alex. Despite the mud and the unfamiliar smells, he became deeply engrossed in the work, his scientific curiosity driving him forward. The machine was a puzzle, and Brian was determined to solve it.

* * *

Brian stood up, brushing dirt off his trousers as he finished a preliminary scan of the machine's interior. "I've checked for any harmful emissions or radiation. So far, everything seems stable and safe," he reported, trying to inject a bit of humour into the serious atmosphere. "I don't think you'll have any mutations or third arms growing."

Alex chuckled, the tension easing slightly. "That's a relief. What else have you found?"

Brian strode over to his equipment, picking up the radio signal detector. "This thing is incredible. It's blocking all radio signals from the outside. It's like a Faraday cage, completely isolating itself from the outside environment. That's why you couldn't get a signal inside."

Alex was intrigued. "So, it's designed to be self-contained. What about its power source? Any idea how it's running?"

"Not yet," Brian admitted. "But it's emitting a consistent electromagnetic field. I haven't detected any traditional power sources like batteries or fuel cells. It could be drawing energy from an unknown source or generating its own, somehow."

Alex frowned, trying to process the information. "And the materials? They seem ... unusual."

Brian agreed enthusiastically. "Exactly. The exterior is composed of a metal alloy that I can't quite identify. It seems incredibly durable and feels unlike any material I've encountered. The interior is even more fascinating—those controls and screens consist of a flexible and resilient substance, almost like a hybrid of metal and plastic. It's truly remarkable."

He opened his notepad, showing Alex the sketches and notes he had been making. "Look at this. As you said, the characters on the controls appear to be a form of Chinese script. I've been documenting the various words and phrases to check them at home later."

Alex examined the notes closely. "Do you have any idea what any of them mean yet?"

Brian took a deep breath, trying to steady his excitement. "Maybe. Look at this," he said, flipping through his notes to a recent page. "I've been working on translating some of the more common sequences of glyphs. Here, this one seems to mean 'coordinate input', and this one 'confirm entry.' It's fascinating—how the symbols are structured suggests a sophisticated interface for inputting destinations, locations, and times."

Alex studied the notepad closely. "So, we might be looking at an advanced navigation system?"

"Exactly," Brian confirmed. "It's like a puzzle, and these glyphs are the pieces. If we can understand how to input coordinates properly, we might be able to control the machine's destinations with more precision. And here's a symbol that I think relates to the machine's power source or readiness state. If we can decipher that, we might get a better handle on how to prepare the machine for a bigger jump."

Alex's eyes widened with realisation. "So, if we decode this, we might be able to tell the machine where and when to go. We could actually navigate this thing to different times and locations of our choice?"

Brian smiled, the thrill of discovery evident in his eyes. "We're making progress, Alex. Slow but steady. It may take a while, but every bit of information brings us closer to mastering this technology."

Alex considered this thoughtfully. "So, where is the machine from? Any theories?"

Brian took a deep breath, considering his words. "Well, based on the design and materials, I'd say this machine is far beyond current human technology. It's sophisticated and carefully engineered. The fact that it can manipulate time, as you've described, suggests an advanced understanding of physics that we haven't yet achieved."

The physicist paused, considering the possibilities. "It could be from the future or developed by a highly advanced civilisation. The isolation from external signals might be a safety feature to prevent interference during time travel."

Alex looked quizzically at Brian. "So, you think it's safe to use again? If so, we need to figure out how to help Ry-Lan and understand what this machine is truly capable of."

Brian thought for a second. "I think it's stable, but we need to be cautious. We should document everything meticulously and proceed step by step. If we're going to use it intentionally, we need to understand exactly what we're dealing with."

As they rested for a moment, Alex reflected on Brian's insights. The serene atmosphere of the farm provided a moment of calm amidst their high-tech investigation. They were still far from understanding the machine's full capabilities, but each discovery brought them closer to the truth.

* * *

Sitting on a couple of large rocks at the edge of the field, Alex and Brian began to discuss their next steps. The tranquil farm setting, with birds chirping and the distant bleating of sheep, provided a soothing backdrop to their intense conversation.

"Brian, do you think we should involve others to help?" Alex asked, looking out over the fields. "There's a lot we still don't understand, and more expertise could be helpful."

Brian took a moment to consider the question. "It's up to you. Involving more people could certainly accelerate our understanding, but it would also involve complications. Once the authorities or more scientists are involved, we would lose all control over the situation. We'd probably never see the machine again."

Alex thought about Brian's statement. "I will have to file a report to my boss, but I can downplay the significance. Make it sound like we're dealing with something minor, a bit of a non-event. That way, we can keep things under wraps for now."

Alex paused, an idea forming in his mind. "If the machine were to 'disappear,' that might simplify things. We could move it to the university where you can access better resources."

Brian shook his head. "Then I might face exactly the same issues you're worried about once my superiors find out."

Alex felt a heavy burden from his responsibilities. "Ry-Lan is still alive, and as long as he is, the machine belongs to him. His message seemed significant and, to be honest, I feel more duty-bound to him than to my job. Once the authorities get more involved, his wishes will be lost in the bureaucracy."

Brian agreed. "You're right. We need to respect Ry-Lan's wishes and handle this delicately. The best course of action might be to try to travel to where Ry-Lan is from. His people might be able to help us understand the machine and his condition better. Plus, we could set up probes inside the machine and film the entire process, so even if we can't find them, we can gather as much data as possible."

Alex was about to speak when his radio crackled to life. "Control to Harper, we've got a traffic collision in Westfield. Can you respond?"

Alex grimaced. "Duty calls. I'll leave you here with the machine, Brian. Can you continue studying the user interface and documenting everything you find?"

"Absolutely. I'll spend the rest of the day here, making notes and trying to decode more of this writing."

"Thanks, Brian. I should also visit the hospital to check on Ry-Lan once I'm done with the incident. We need to keep an eye on his condition."

As Alex turned to leave, he suddenly remembered the card for the machine. "Sorry, Brian, I nearly went off with this," he said, reaching into his pocket and handing it to Brian.

"Thanks, mate. See you soon," Brian replied with a smile.

As Alex headed towards his car, he felt relief and anticipation. They had a plan, and while the path ahead was uncertain, he was determined to uncover the truth about the mysterious machine and Ry-Lan's urgent message.

* * *

Brian watched as Alex drove off, leaving him alone with the machine. The early afternoon sun hung low in the sky, casting long shadows across the farm. He took a deep breath, the air filled with the scent of grass and the faint hum of the machine. The tranquillity of the surroundings was at odds with the complex task before him.

He took out his notepad and phone again, ready to tackle more of the machine's user interface. Brian had always been methodical, and this situation called for his most meticulous approach. He climbed back into the machine, the interior becoming slowly familiar but still mysterious.

Inside, the soft ambient lighting cast a glow over the controls. Brian sat in the chair, scanning the array of touchscreens and buttons. He opened the translation app on his phone, ready to decode more of the enigmatic writing. He started by photographing the screens, ensuring he had clear images of each symbol and sequence.

Brian focused on a set of characters he hadn't examined closely before. He held his phone up to the screen, using the camera to capture the symbols and translate them in real time. The translations were often rough and required some interpretation but provided a starting point. He jotted down the results in his notepad, creating a reference guide for the various commands.

Brian's notepad quickly filled with sketches and notes, each page a step closer to understanding the machine. He carefully documented each symbol and its potential meaning, cross-referencing them with previous observations. The more he worked, the clearer the interface became. The glyphs weren't just random; they obviously formed a coherent system.

Hours passed as Brian continued his meticulous study. Occasionally, he would step outside the machine to stretch his legs and clear his mind, the farm's peaceful surroundings providing a brief respite before he returned to his task. Each time he re-entered the machine, he felt renewed determination.

Brian felt hungry as his stomach rumbled now and then. He wished he had packed some food, a blunder he made in his hurry to collect equipment, a mistake that made the day feel even longer.

Brian was making steady progress. He had identified several key symbols and their functions, creating a rudimentary understanding of the machine's interface. He still had many questions, but the framework began taking shape. Deciding to take a break and review his findings, Brian sat outside the machine, his notepad in hand, and began to organise his notes. The challenge was immense, but he felt a growing sense of excitement. The machine was revealing its secrets, one symbol at a time.

He knew there was still much to learn, but each discovery made the path forward more apparent. The machine's capabilities were extraordinary, and understanding its interface was the key to unlocking its full potential. He wondered when Alex would return. He was looking forward to sharing his findings with Alex and discussing what they might do next.

Chapter 7

Alex arrived at the accident scene, his blue lights flashing as he pulled up. It had been at least twenty-five minutes since the incident occurred, and the drivers were already out of their vehicles, looking frustrated and cold. A delivery van had swerved to avoid a dog, crashing into a lamppost, while a small hatchback had collided with the van's rear, creating a traffic jam on the town's main road.

As Alex stepped out of his car, the first raindrops began to fall, quickly turning into a steady downpour. He approached the drivers, assessing their conditions. Both were shaken but uninjured. The van driver, a middle-aged man with a worried expression, was pacing beside his vehicle while the hatchback's driver, a young woman, frantically talked on her phone.

"Is everyone alright here?" Alex asked, raising his voice over the rain.

"Yes, Officer, just a bit shaken up," the van driver replied. "I didn't see the dog until it was too late."

"I'm okay, too," the young woman responded, putting her phone away. "But I need to try to get home. I have a babysitter waiting for me."

"We'll sort this out," Alex assured them. "I need to get your contact details."

The recovery service had already been called and was on its way. Alex set about ensuring the scene was safe. He directed the drivers to the side and set up traffic cones, ensuring the road remained safe for passing traffic. The rain was relentless, but Alex was grateful for his police waterproof jacket and hat, which kept him mostly dry.

While he worked, Alex's thoughts drifted back to the farm. He wondered how Brian was managing with the machine in this weather. He hadn't said goodbye to Tommy before leaving and hoped Tommy had checked on Brian. The rain was coming down harder now, and Alex couldn't help but picture Brian alone in the field, dealing with the high-tech machine amidst the mud and dampness.

After securing the scene and waiting for the recovery vehicles to arrive, Alex stood by the side of the road, directing traffic around the accident. The tailback slowly began to ease as vehicles were guided past the obstruction. Alex's mind, though, remained divided between his duties here and the mysteries back at the farm.

* * *

It seemed hours since Brian had watched Alex's car disappear down the muddy track, leaving him alone with the enigmatic machine. The rain had begun to fall steadily, creating a soft patter on the machine's exterior and soaking the ground around it. Despite the cold and damp, Brian felt growing excitement. He was determined to make the most of this once-in-a-lifetime opportunity.

Before continuing his examination, Brian realised he needed to relieve the pressure from his bladder. It had been building for a while, but now it could wait no more. Stepping away from the machine, he found a discreet spot against one of the nearby walls, ensuring he was respectful of the surroundings. The momentary pause allowed him to gather his thoughts and refocus on the task ahead.

He climbed back into the machine, trying to carefully wipe the mud from his shoes as he stepped inside. The interior was dry and softly lit. Brian took a moment to adjust his eyes to the ambient lighting and settled into the chair in front of the control panel.

Pulling out his notepad and phone, Brian resumed his meticulous study of the user interface. Using the translation app, he methodically documented the command options, taking photos of the screens and translating the words in real time. The translations often required some interpretation but provided a starting point. He jotted down the results in his notepad, cross-referencing them with previous observations.

Brian's systematic approach paid off as he discovered a new set of symbols related to the machine's video system. He found a menu that allowed him to access external cameras. Intrigued, he selected the option and watched as the screens switched, displaying a panoramic view from around the machine. The cameras were incredibly well-hidden, invisible to the naked eye from the outside.

Determined to locate the cameras precisely, Brian searched for anything he could use to mark their positions. He wanted to use tape or something similar but couldn't find anything suitable. Finally, he devised a creative solution. Going outside, he began smearing mud on various parts of the machine's surface. Eventually, he found the small, nearly imperceptible lenses. He cleaned the mud off, impressed once more by the machine's advanced design and the seamless integration of its components.

Brian knew he had made significant progress. By the time Alex finally returned, he would have so much to tell him. He had identified several components and their functions, creating a rudimentary understanding of the machine's interface. He documented everything meticulously. As the rain continued falling outside, Brian felt a growing anticipation for where it would lead them.

* * *

Meanwhile, Alex had finished at the traffic accident and had driven through the familiar streets towards the hospital, his mind spinning about the day's events and the perplexing machine. After arriving at the hospital, he went through the bustling corridors to Ry-Lan's room. The sterile smell of disinfectant filled the air.

Dr Zayn greeted him as he approached. "Sergeant Harper, good to see you again. You're here to check on our mystery patient, I assume? Do you have any information yet for us about his identity?"

"No, I'm sorry." Alex didn't know what to tell the doctor. "We're still trying hard to find out who he is. But all our enquiries have drawn a blank so far."

"OK, well, we really need something to work with."

"I understand. But it's complicated. We think he might be a soldier or diplomat, something of that nature," Alex replied, "so we need to keep this matter confidential. Can you do that for me?"

"Of course." Dr Zayn seemed excited by the prospect.

Alex quickly wanted to change the subject. He looked through the observation window at Ry-Lan, lying motionless but stable. "How's he doing?"

Dr Zayn sighed, looking at the monitors that displayed Ry-Lan's vital signs. "He's stable but still unconscious. We've been monitoring him closely, and some interesting developments have occurred."

Alex was intrigued. "Interesting developments?"

"Yes," Dr Zayn continued. "We've noticed REM-like eye movements, which suggest that he might be dreaming or in a deep sleep. His implants appear to be actively supporting him, too. They seem to be aiding his body in maintaining stable functions, possibly even enhancing his healing processes."

Looking away from Ry-Lan, Alex asked, "So, what's the plan?"

Dr Zayn met his gaze. "Given the unique nature of his condition and the implants, we've decided to limit our medical intervention. We're focusing on monitoring him closely, allowing his body—and whatever those implants are doing—to maintain his health. It's a cautious approach, but we believe it's the best course of action for now."

Alex appreciated the careful consideration. "Thank you, Doctor. Please keep me updated on any changes."

"Of course, Sergeant," Dr Zayn replied. "We'll let you know immediately if there's any change in his condition."

* * *

As Alex left the hospital, he felt relief and determination. Ry-Lan was stable, but so many unanswered questions remained. He strode briskly to his car, keen to return to the farm. He got into the driver's seat and had just buckled his seatbelt when his radio crackled to life.

"Control to Harper, we have a shoplifting incident at the off-licence in Lower Helmworth. Can you respond?"

Alex sighed inwardly. "Roger that, Control. I'm on my way," he replied, starting the engine and heading towards Lower Helmworth.

By the time Alex arrived at the shop, the clouds had cleared, and the sun was finally visible. It was low and cast an orange hue over the town. Alex parked his car and walked into the off-licence, where the shopkeeper, Mr Harris, greeted him with a look of recognition.

"Good to see you, Sergeant Harper," Mr Harris said, frustration and resignation in his expression. "It's that Jenkins lad again. Caught him trying to steal a bottle of vodka. When I confronted him, he ran off with it."

Alex knew exactly who Mr Harris was talking about. The "Jenkins boy", Peter, had been in trouble several times before, but it was usually for minor pranks, not theft. "Did you see which way he went?" Alex asked.

"Down Maple Street, then he disappeared into the alley," Mr Harris replied. "I would have chased after him, but my legs aren't what they used to be."

"Thanks, Mr Harris. I'll handle it from here," Alex assured him. He left the store and walked down Maple Street towards the alley, scanning for any sign of Peter. Once through the alley, he approached the Jenkins' house. He noticed the lights were off, and there was no movement inside.

Alex knocked on the door and waited, but there was no response. He knocked again, louder this time, but still nothing. It seemed that no one was home. He made a mental note to return later and have a word with Peter and his parents.

With nothing more he could do, Alex got back into his car and headed back towards the farm. The sky was cloudy once again, suggesting rain. The day had been long and filled with distractions, but Alex's mind had kept drifting back to the mysterious machine and Brian's ongoing investigation.

When Alex finally arrived back at the farm, he was greeted by the sight of Brian sitting by the machine, looking tired but pleased to see him. Brian stood up and stretched, smiling wearily.

"Welcome back," Brian said. "How did it go?"

"Busy with work," Alex replied, shaking his head. "Though I did manage to get to the hospital. How about you? Any new discoveries?"

"Yes." Brian's eyes lit up despite his fatigue. "I've made some progress. Let's go over everything while it's still fresh in my mind."

Alex smiled, feeling a sense of camaraderie and renewed purpose. "I'll tell you what. Let's head to The Plough instead and talk over a beer. I'm off duty now."

Brian's face brightened at the suggestion. "Great. I could use a change of scenery and a drink."

They packed up their gear and headed to The Plough, back towards Helmworth. The pub was bustling with evening patrons, but Alex found a quiet corner where they could talk undisturbed. They ordered their drinks and some food and settled into a booth.

When the two men finally sat down with a drink in their hands, Alex felt relieved. Despite the long and challenging day, the familiar setting of the pub and the presence of a good friend brought him comfort. "So, what did you find out?" he asked, sipping his beer.

Chapter 8

The pub provided a perfect backdrop for their discussion, with its rustic charm and low murmur of conversation.

Brian pulled out his notebook filled with copious notes and sketches and showed it to Alex. "I've been working on pinpointing the origin point Ry-Lan came from before you first met him. Based on my calculations, it's somewhere near to this destination."

Alex's eyes widened. "Really? That's interesting. And do you know when he originated from?"

Brian turned the pages, showing Alex the detailed coordinates. "Again, if I've understood it correctly, the difference is minimal. I think Ry-Lan came from about two weeks in the future."

The implications of the words echoed in Alex's mind, charged with potential. He wanted to ensure that he understood, "So you think Ry-Lan travelled first to somewhere nearby, a fortnight in the future, and then travelled back to Tommy's field where I saw him?"

"Exactly. The proximity in time and location suggests that Ry-Lan's journey was intentional. But I think the bigger question is why he ended up at Tommy's farm."

Alex lowered his voice, ensuring no one was listening. "What do you think his purpose was? Why choose a remote farm in Yorkshire?"

Brian considered this possibility, "It could be that he was looking for a place where he wouldn't be immediately discovered. A farm like Tommy's is isolated enough to avoid drawing attention."

"True," Alex agreed, "but there surely has to be more to it. Maybe Tommy's farm was a meeting point, or perhaps Ry-Lan was searching for something specific in this area."

Brian tapped his pen on the table, deep in thought. "If Ry-Lan came from the future, he might well have known where and when it would be safe to land. Tommy's farm could have been identified as a low-risk location."

"Or," Alex added, "he might have been trying to avoid someone or something. Maybe he was in trouble and thought the farm would be a good hiding place."

Brian considered this for a second. "That's a possibility too. We also need to consider why Ry-Lan first travelled to the spot ten days from now. There must be a reason for that stop, too. What exactly did Ry-Lan say when he spoke to you? Did he give any clues about why he was here?"

Alex paused, recalling the conversation. "He wanted me to record him giving a message, but it was in a language I couldn't understand. It sounded Chinese-like, and a doctor at the hospital who speaks Chinese was able to translate some of it. He told me that Ry-Lan mentioned 'family,' 'water,' and possibly 'disease.'"

Brian's brow furrowed. "Family, water, disease ... That's cryptic but intriguing. Maybe he was trying to warn us about something or seeking help."

The weight of their discussion settled over them as they thought for a while. Alex glanced around the pub again, checking no one could hear him. "Brian, I think I should make another jump. I want to travel to Ry-Lan's previous destination."

Brian's face softened, showing the conflict in his eyes. "I don't know, Alex. It's risky. We still don't fully understand how this machine works."

"I know," Alex replied firmly. "But we need to know more. If I can understand what Ry-Lan was doing, or perhaps travel to where Ry-Lan is from, then maybe we can understand this machine better—and help him, too. And we need to get on with it."

Brian sighed, then agreed, too tired to argue. "Alright. Let's get a good night's sleep, and then first thing tomorrow, we'll do it."

* * *

Brian drove home, their conversation pressing heavily on his mind. He knew it was risky, but Alex was determined, and they did want to make progress. As he pulled into his driveway, seeing his home brought him back to normality.

Meanwhile, Alex returned to his house, the events of the evening replaying in his mind, too. Sleep was elusive that night as thoughts of the upcoming jump and its potential dangers governed his mind. He tossed and turned, unable to quiet his racing thoughts.

The hours dragged on, and exhaustion finally began to take its toll. When Alex eventually drifted off, his sleep was far from restful. He began to dream, transported to the hot and arid environment of the

Middle East. The air was thick and stifling, the oppressive heat bearing down on him.

In the dream, everything felt muted and distant, as if viewed through a haze. He saw his brother in the distance, his heart leaping with hope and desperation. "Mark!" he called out, his voice muffled and weak. He started to run towards his brother, but with every step he took, Mark seemed to move further away, the distance between them growing insurmountable.

"Mark, wait!" Alex shouted, his voice barely carrying over the dull roar of indistinct noises in the background. He pushed himself to run faster, but no matter how hard he tried, he couldn't close the gap. His brother turned to look at him, smiling, but didn't say a word. The scene around Alex began to blur even more, the sense of helplessness washing over him.

He awoke with a start, his heart pounding and sweat drenching his sheets. The nightmare left him shaken, the unresolved anguish over his brother's fate resurfacing with brutal clarity. As dawn's first light began to seep through his curtains, Alex forced himself out of bed, his body weary but his resolve stronger than ever.

Determined, he prepared for the day ahead. Despite the poor sleep, he knew what needed to be done. The drive to Tommy's farm was cloaked in the usual morning mist, with the air crisp and cool. He arrived at the farm to find Brian already there, setting up the equipment needed for the jump.

Sat 6th April 2024

As it was a Saturday and he was not at work, Alex had chosen to wear his regular clothes instead of his police uniform. The casual attire made him feel a bit more relaxed, without the heavy weight of his police jacket and all the paraphernalia he had to wear for work.

Tommy spotted Alex pulling up, and he walked over with concern. He noticed Alex's different look and asked, "Alex, what brings you here today? I didn't think you work on weekends."

Alex offered a reassuring smile. "You're right, Tommy. But this can't wait. It's too important to leave, even on my day off."

Tommy chewed his lip. "Urgent, huh? OK. But what if this machine starts attracting the wrong kind of attention? Government types or those conspiracy crowds? Could disturb more than just the sheep, you know."

Alex looked Tommy in the eyes, appreciating his fears. "Tommy, I hear you. But it's just us here, and everything's under control. We're not planning on making this a spectacle."

Tommy reluctantly accepted Alex's response. "Alright, I'm counting on you to keep it quiet. Just don't let this thing turn my farm into a circus."

With his point made, Tommy walked back towards the barn, leaving Alex to continue his preparations. Alex watched him go back inside, then turned to find Brian adjusting a complex array of monitoring equipment laid out systematically near the machine.

"Good morning, Brian. How are you doing?" Alex asked, approaching the setup.

Brian looked up and smiled. "Good, thanks. I thought I'd get an early start."

"Thanks for coming out so soon. I really appreciate it."

"Almost there," Brian replied, still focused on his task. "I've prepped the machine for Ry-Lan's previous destination, but before I lock it in, let's run through the return sequence together. I want to make sure you're familiar with the steps."

Alex agreed. "Sounds good. I'm ready." Resolutely, he stepped into the machine once more, re-familiarizing himself with its controls as Brian guided him through the return sequence. They practiced each step together, ensuring Alex could handle the process on his own.

"I've made you a printed copy of the return sequence," Brian instructed, handing Alex a small piece of paper that he had laminated with the detailed instructions. "Follow these steps exactly to ensure you can come back. We can't risk any mistakes."

"Got it," Alex confirmed, studying the sheet intently. "Let's go through it now one more time."

After a thorough rehearsal, Brian was satisfied with Alex's understanding. "Alright, now that you're clear, I'll set the destination. When you're ready, just hit this here. It means 'accept'."

Satisfied and feeling more confident after their practice, Alex settled into his chair while the machine hummed invitingly around him. With

Alex ready, Brian returned to the monitoring setup a few metres away, from where he could best observe. Alex hovered his hand over the activation buttons, his heart racing with anticipation and slight anxiety.

"I'm ready," Alex said, checking his bodycam and glancing back at Brian, who smiled reassuringly. "Should we count down or something?"

Brian chuckled softly. "I think you should close the door first, then we can go for the dramatic countdown."

Laughing, Alex operated the door closure mechanism, sealing himself inside. The machine's interior became quieter, with the sounds from outside muffled by the closed door.

"Okay, here goes nothing. Three ... two ... one," Alex murmured, pressing the 'accept' button. The machine's noise grew louder, its lights flickering as it powered up, ready to transport him to the unknown. The sequence was becoming more familiar to him, each jump feeling more intuitive than the last.

Chapter 9

Sat 20th April 2024

The machine came to a halt, the hum and vibrations gradually fading. Alex felt the familiar sensation of the journey ending, anticipation and anxiety coursing through him. He took a deep breath, opened the hatch, and stepped out into the cool night air.

He glanced around, trying to get his bearings. It was dark, and his eyes needed to adjust. It seemed he had landed in a car park. Not far away was a large sports stadium, currently unused and shrouded in darkness. The whole area felt deserted, with only the occasional streetlight breaking the monotony. A distant hum of traffic and the soft, constant patter of rain created an eerie quiet, adding to the sense of isolation.

Alex took a moment to take it all in. He noticed the slick, wet tarmac and the faint glow of streetlights reflecting off puddles. The stadium loomed large and silent in the distance, its darkened structure towering over the empty parking lot. A stream and trees bordered one side of the car park.

It took a moment to adjust to the environment. The journey had been smooth, but Alex had to figure out where he was and what to do next. As he continued to survey the area, he remained vigilant, his senses heightened. The light rain began to soak through his clothes, but he barely noticed, focused on his task. Alex knew he needed to stay alert and be ready for anything.

Then, Alex's attention was drawn to a nearby car he hadn't noticed. He heard a click as the car door opened.

The car's interior light revealed a man stepping out of the vehicle. He was of average build, with very short gingery hair and freckles. The man wore a chunky, gold-looking chain around his neck. He approached Alex quickly, clearly agitated.

"Hey! Who are you? What are you doing in that thing, and where is the other guy?" the man demanded, his voice carrying a noticeable northern accent laced with confusion and hostility.

Alex, taken aback by the figure's aggression, tried to deflect his questions. "I don't know who you saw, but I just arrived here myself."

The man narrowed his eyes, clearly not convinced. "Don't lie to me. Something's not right here."

Sensing the situation could escalate, Alex remained calm but alert. "Look, let's not make this worse. We can talk and figure out what's happening together."

The aggressor was having none of it. He glanced around and spotted a broken fence post lying on the ground. Suddenly, he picked it up and brandished it threateningly at Alex.

"Stay back!" Alex commanded, his voice firm and authoritative. "I'm a police officer. Let's just calm down and talk this through."

The man swung the fence post at Alex, who ducked and leapt to the side, narrowly avoiding the blow.

"Put that down and step back!" Alex repeated, trying to maintain control.

The man swung again, and this time, Alex managed to grab his arm, using his momentum to throw the man off balance. He struggled to grip the wet pavement, his feet slipping as they grappled. In the tussle, the man fell, and his head hit the ground with a sickening thud, knocking him unconscious.

* * *

Alex quickly glanced around, the sense of urgency increasing. He knelt, feeling the rain soak through his clothes, and checked the man's pulse, relieved to find it strong and steady. Searching the man's pockets, he found a wallet. Flipping it open, he found a driver's licence identifying the man as Ian Cooper, from the Linthorpe area of Middlesbrough.

Alex took a photo of the ID with his phone, the flash briefly illuminating the man's unconscious face, before putting it back into his pocket.

With the ID safely documented, Alex stood up, the rain running down his face as he scanned the area. He then took a photo of the man, hoping it would be useful later.

As he pondered his next move, Ian began to regain consciousness, groaning softly. Alex felt a pang of uncertainty. Events were becoming more dangerous by the second. Deciding he couldn't risk further confrontation, Alex hurried back to the machine, closing the hatch behind him. And, sliding into the machine's familiar confines, he activated the return procedure.

The machine hummed to life, the usual vibrations signalling the start of the return trip. Alex took a deep breath, trying to steady his nerves. The surroundings outside the machine blurred as he was transported back to the farm.

Sat 6th April 2024

The machine came to a halt, the hum and vibrations fading away. Alex took a moment to steady himself before opening the hatch. Stepping out into the familiar surroundings of Tommy's farm, he felt a wave of relief wash over him. The adrenaline still coursing through his veins made his hands tremble slightly. Brian was waiting nearby, his expression hinting at curiosity and concern.

"Alex, what happened?" Brian asked and then noticed the dampness of Alex's clothes. "Why are you wet?"

"I'm okay. Just a bit shaken up, and it was raining there," Alex responded, trying to steady his voice.

Brian blinked, trying to process what Alex had said. "Wait, what? It worked? You travelled? I've only just said goodbye to you. How is that possible?"

Alex took a deep breath, understanding Brian's scepticism. "Yes, I've been gone for a good five minutes. It took me to a car park near a large stadium. It was nighttime and raining. As I was getting my bearings, a man confronted me. I think he must have seen Ry-Lan go into the machine and was surprised to see me come out instead."

Brian's eyes widened. "Then what happened?"

Alex recounted the episode, describing the man's initial hostility and how it escalated into violence. He explained how the man had picked up a fence post and attacked him, and how he had used his police training to subdue the aggressor, accidentally knocking him unconscious in the process. Brian listened intently, his concern growing with each detail.

"I checked his ID," Alex continued. "His name is Ian Cooper, and he lives in Middlesbrough. I took a photo of his driving licence. When Ian started to come around, I knew I had to get out of there. So, I followed the return procedure and came home."

Brian shook his head in disbelief. "It's hard to get my head around this. But it sounds like a dangerous encounter. If we do this again, we must be more prepared next time."

Alex, his mind still reeling from the experience, agreed. "Yes, totally. I don't want to get into that kind of problem again."

Alex took a deep breath, trying to steady himself after the encounter. "If I'm honest, I didn't really think it through. I had no real plan for dealing with any threats."

Brian contemplated Alex's words. "We need to be more careful. If we're going to keep doing this, we've got to anticipate these kinds of predicaments. Maybe you should consider taking some form of self-defence with you on future jumps."

Alex agreed, "You're right."

Brian suggested, "What about pepper spray? It's non-lethal but effective."

Alex thought for a moment and then said, "Actually, we use PAVA spray now. It's similar to pepper spray but safer. Yes, I think that's a good shout."

The conversation shifted as they felt the pressure of time weighing down on them. "We can't afford to rush into another jump without being fully prepared," Alex said. "But at the same time, we have to act quickly. There's so much at stake."

Brian's tired eyes showed just how heavily he felt about their situation. "I know. We need more information before we make another jump. Let's take today to regroup, gather what we need, and plan our next steps carefully."

As they finalised their plans, the significance of the unknown challenges ahead loomed large. Both men felt the immense pressure and the urgency of their mission, but they were also determined to proceed with more caution and preparation. The future was uncertain, but they knew they had to face it head-on.

Chapter 10

Alex shivered as the chilly morning air seeped through his damp clothes. "Let's get in my car and warm up," he suggested, motioning towards his parked vehicle.

Brian agreed, and they walked over to Alex's car. Once inside, Alex sparked the ignition and cranked up the heater. The warmth quickly began reaching his bones, relieving the outside chill.

Brian reached into his bag and pulled out a thermos. "I brought some tea," he said, unscrewing the lid and pouring two cups. "I learned my lesson from yesterday. Thought it would be a good idea to come better prepared."

Alex took the offered cup, grateful for the warmth it brought. "Thanks, Brian. This is exactly what I needed."

They sat silently for a few moments, sipping their tea and enjoying the respite from the cold outside. Alex felt the tension from his recent experience slowly easing.

Brian then delved into his bag again and drew out his laptop. "I think we should review the

bodycam footage," he said, taking the SD card from the bodycam and inserting it into the laptop. "Let's see exactly what happened in that car park."

Alex edged closer to get a better view of the screen. The footage played, showing Alex's arrival at the car park, his initial observations, and the sudden confrontation with the man. It was difficult to see well, given the poor light. So, Brian paused the video at various points to try to get a better look.

"You know," Brian said, "the machine has external cameras. We could also review the footage from those. Plus, next time, you could use them to survey the area first."

"I didn't think of that. That could definitely be useful."

Brian continued, "You can watch the camera feeds on the screens inside the machine before stepping out. That way, you'll better understand what's outside before you step into another potential confrontation."

Alex felt encouraged by Brian's suggestions. "That's a great idea. We need every advantage we can get."

* * *

With the car heater on and tea warming them up, Alex and Brian continued their discussion.

"Here," Alex said, pulling out his phone. "Here is the photo of the guy's ID." He handed the phone to Brian, who studied the image.

"Hmm. Ian Cooper," Brian noted. "Do you recognise him at all?"

Alex shook his head. "No, I've never seen him before. But he was definitely expecting someone else to come out of the machine. He seemed really confused when he saw me."

Brian looked thoughtful. "What about the location? Did you manage to get any accurate GPS data?"

Alex sighed. "I didn't think to check while I was there. I was too focused on dealing with Ian. Maybe we could try to figure it out from the video."

Brian's eyes lit up. "Hey, what about the photo? Check its metadata. Maybe the location data was recorded with it."

Alex opened the photo on his phone and accessed the details. A smile spread across his face as he found the location data. "Got it. Look, it's mapped out here! It's Mowden Park rugby stadium in Darlington."

Brian settled back into his seat, contemplating Alex's words. "Alright, that gives us a specific location. Now we need to figure out why Ian was there and why he was expecting to see Ry-Lan."

Alex frowned, thinking. "Maybe he was just drawn to the machine's appearance and thought it was valuable or important. He might have been trying to use or learn more about it. It's not like you come across one of these every day."

Alex paused, drumming his fingers on the dashboard. "Unfortunately, I can't investigate Ian's background without going into work, and I don't want to do that today to avoid raising any suspicion."

Brian understood. "That makes sense. But at least we have a starting point with the location. Maybe we can find out more by visiting the car park in Darlington?"

Alex agreed. "It's a good idea. We'll need to gather more clues and see if we can piece together why Ian was there and what he knows about Ry-Lan."

They sat in momentary silence, their circumstances bearing down on them. They had made limited progress, but so many unanswered questions remained.

* * *

As the car's warmth and the tea fortified them, Alex decided to share something else playing on his mind. Biting his lip, he turned to his friend. "Brian, there's something else I need to tell you." Lowering his voice with the gravity he felt, he added, "Last night, I had a dream about my brother, Mark."

Brian looked at Alex, reading his discomfort. "Go on," he prompted.

Alex sighed, the memory of the dream still vivid. "I was in the desert. I saw Mark in the distance, and I tried to reach him, but no matter how fast I ran, he kept getting further away. It was like he was just out of reach, and I couldn't help him."

Brian listened intently, the depth of Alex's emotional turmoil apparent. "Why are you telling me this, Alex?"

Alex looked away. "Because I feel like I failed him. And now, with this machine, I keep thinking ... maybe I could go back and find out what happened to him. Maybe I could help him."

Brian's expression turned sombre. After a long, drawn-out breath, he said, "Alex, I understand why you'd want to do that. But travelling back to a war zone is damned risky. One – you might not be able to come back, and two – the machine could fall into the wrong hands."

Alex looked down as Brian's words sunk in. "I know it's risky, but I can't shake the feeling that I need to try. I owe it to Mark to find out what happened to him if nothing else."

Brian shook his head, the movement showing his frustration. "But what about Ry-Lan? You've been so focused on helping him, and now it seems like your priorities are shifting."

Alex took a deep breath, trying to reconcile his conflicting emotions. "I'm sorry, Brian. I do want to help Ry-Lan, but the thought of not knowing what happened to Mark still tears me apart. How can I ignore it, when I may have the chance to help him?"

Brian understood the depth of Alex's dilemma. "I get it, Alex. It's a lot to handle. But we need to be smart about this. If you go back to find him and something happens to you, we'll lose the machine and our chance to help Ry-Lan."

Despite Brian's words, Alex's eyes filled with determination, his expression resolute. "I can't live with the regret of not trying. If I don't do this, I'll never forgive myself. But I promise I'll be careful. I'll make sure the machine doesn't fall into the wrong hands."

Brian sighed, picking up on Alex's stance and knowing there was no easy answer. "Alright, Alex. Just promise me we'll think this through carefully before making any decisions. We can't afford any mistakes."

Relieved at Brian's understanding, Alex slapped his friend on the shoulder. "I promise, Brian. We'll figure this out together."

They sat in silence for a moment, deep in communal contemplation. Despite the risks, Alex felt energised and had a renewed sense of purpose. He knew what he had to do but also knew he couldn't do it alone.

* * *

"Let's head to Darlington," Alex suggested. "We can check out the car park and the surrounding area. Maybe we'll find some clues about this guy Cooper or why he was there."

Brian agreed. "It's a good idea. Plus, we can pick up some supplies while we're there. We need to be better prepared for any future jumps."

They quickly gathered their things and drove towards Darlington, their conversation allowing them to plan and strategize. The journey took about 25 minutes, giving them plenty of time to discuss their next steps.

"What do you think we'll find when we reach the car park?" Alex asked, glancing over at Brian as he drove.

Brian chewed his lip. "We have to remember we're two weeks ahead of your encounter with Ian. There might not be anything obvious yet, but it's important to get a lay of the land. Maybe we can find some clues about why he was there or if he's been watching the area."

"Good point," Alex replied. "Fingers crossed we find something useful. Even small details could help us understand what's going on."

As they neared Darlington, they continued speculating about what they might find. Alex mentioned they should look for any signs of surveillance or unusual activity. Brian suggested checking out nearby businesses or talking to locals to see if anyone had noticed anything strange.

Anticipation and uncertainty affected them both, aware that this visit could be crucial in uncovering more about the mysterious circumstances surrounding Ry-Lan and Ian Cooper. The need to act quickly and effectively drove them to make the most of their time.

Chapter 11

As the morning sun climbed in the sky, Alex and Brian approached the Mowden Park stadium's expansive car park in Darlington. The area was relatively empty, with only a few vehicles scattered around. A mid-morning calm hung over the place, its quietness mirroring the stillness Alex had experienced during his nocturnal visit, albeit under a different context.

Parking the car, they stepped out, taking in the surroundings. A gentle stream murmured to one side of the car park, flanked by a line of mature trees swaying idly in the breeze. This serene boundary marked the edge of the car park where Alex had appeared from the future—a detail he indicated to Brian as they headed towards that exact spot.

"The car park was almost empty like this when I arrived that night," Alex remarked, scanning the area with a critical eye. "It felt eerie, being here with the stadium looming over me, completely dark and silent."

Brian nodded as his gaze swept over the quiet tarmac. "I bet this place gets pretty busy on match days," he mused.

They slowly walked the area's perimeter where Alex had emerged, searching for any sign indicating anything unusual.

As they reached the precise location where Alex believed he had exited the machine, he stopped and looked around. The ground was just wet asphalt, the regular kind you'd find in any car park, with no markings to suggest anything out of the ordinary might occur.

"This is it, right here," he said, pointing to a spot on the ground. "This is where I stepped out into the future. It's weird, knowing that in a couple of weeks, I'll be standing right here again under very different circumstances."

Brian, who had been quietly observing the surroundings, finally spoke up. "It's good to get a feel for the place in daylight. Helps us get our bearings and maybe even anticipate what could go wrong when you return."

* * *

As Alex and Brian stood at the edge of the car park, the air hung heavy with expectation. The place seemed deceptively quiet, the kind of quiet that hinted at secrets lying just beneath the surface.

Brian looked around, arms raised in emphasis on how mundane it seemed. "There really is nothing special here. Nothing at all," he murmured.

Alex heaved a frustrated breath, turning around and pointing. "Let's check the stream and the trees again. Maybe there's something we've missed."

They paced over to where the stream ran. The water flowed quietly, its surface reflecting the sunlight through the branches. Alex scanned the area, his gaze moving methodically from the trees to the water and back again. Still, nothing unusual stirred their interest.

Alex sighed, the possibility of an unusual occurrence still gnawing at him. "Alright, let's walk the perimeter of the car park. Maybe we'll find something there."

They began a slow circuit around the car park, Alex's eyes sharp as they moved. He noted the positions of the CCTV cameras.

"These cameras," Alex said, pointing them out to Brian, "they cover the entrance and that section near the stadium. But look," he continued, gesturing towards the part of the car park where the machine had appeared, "there's nothing covering that spot. It's a blind spot."

Brian nodded, understanding dawning in his eyes. "So, whatever happened, it was right in the one place the cameras can't see."

"Exactly," Alex replied, his frustration giving way to a sense of clarity. "I think it may be intentional."

They continued their perimeter walk, but the rest of the area yielded no further clues. With its neatly painted lines and occasional cars, the car park remained stubbornly ordinary despite the extraordinary events Alex knew would occur.

Alex felt a chill that had nothing to do with the cool breeze. "So, what now?"

* * *

As Alex and Brian continued their examination of the car park, footsteps approached from behind. They turned to see a car park attendant closing up on them, his lowered eyebrows suggesting curiosity and mild suspicion. The man wore a luminous jacket that stood out against the dull car park.

"Morning, gents," the attendant greeted them. "Can I help you? Are you here for the game? It's not until 3 o'clock."

Alex, always quick on his feet, offered a reassuring smile. "Morning. I'm Sergeant Alex Harper with the North Yorkshire Constabulary. I wasn't aware of a match today. But I am interested to know if there is a game on two weeks from today?"

The attendant relaxed slightly, though his curiosity was still piqued. "Ah, I see. Always good to have the police here. We get all sorts around here on match days. Yes, we're home again in two weeks' time – against Moseley."

Brian chimed in, aiming to keep the conversation casual. "Must be a busy place on game days. How's the turnout usually?"

"Pretty good," the attendant replied, glancing around the car park as if imagining it filled with cars and fans. "Especially for the big matches. Keeps us on our toes."

Alex steered the conversation towards their real interest. He pulled out his phone and showed the attendant a photo of Ian's driving licence. "By the way, we're also looking for someone. Have you seen this man around? Maybe at a past event?"

The attendant squinted at the photo, scratching his head. "Hmm, he does look a bit familiar, but I can't be sure. We get so many faces through here, it's hard to keep track."

Alex kept his tone friendly, though he felt a hint of frustration. "Anything you remember could help. Did he do anything that stood out?"

The attendant shook his head slowly. "Sorry, mate. Nothing comes to mind right now."

"Thanks, I appreciate it," Alex said, slipping his phone back into his pocket. "We'll be around for a bit longer, just wrapping things up."

The attendant gave a small wave before heading back towards his post. Alex watched him go, the brief interaction having been inconclusive.

"At least we know the man might have been seen here before," Brian said, trying to find the silver lining. "It's a start."

Alex sighed, the mystery continuing to deepen. "Yeah, it's something, I suppose. Let's keep looking around. Maybe there's more to find."

* * *

As Alex and Brian stood by the car park, the reality of their situation hardly needed clarifying. The car park attendant's shallow recognition wasn't enough to lead them to any concrete answers about the man Alex had seen.

"Well, that didn't give us much to go on," Brian remarked, frustration edging his voice.

"No, it didn't," Alex agreed. "We have no solid leads on this guy. The attendant's vague recognition is barely a thread."

Brian stroked a smooth palm across his chin. "We need to be better prepared for any future encounters. Maybe we should gather some equipment to help us handle whatever comes next."

Alex agreed. "Yes, where should we start?"

Brian pulled out his phone and searched for a nearby outdoor supply store. After a few moments, he found one. "There's an outdoor gear store not too far from here. It should have some useful things for us."

"Perfect," Alex replied. "Let's head over there."

They drove to the store, discussing what they might need. Upon arriving, they ducked inside, greeted by rows of outdoor equipment. Alex grabbed a rucksack and started filling it with handy items: a first aid kit, water purification tablets, a mini toolkit, an elastic cord, a spare wallet, a battery-operated radio, a blanket, energy bars, and duct tape.

"We need to be ready for anything," Alex said, checking off items from his mental list. "We can't afford to be caught off guard again."

Brian picked up a few additional items, including a portable charger and a small flashlight. "We should also consider setting up some basic surveillance equipment. Maybe some cameras we can hide near the car park."

"Good idea," Alex agreed. "We'll look into that once we're back and more settled."

They paid for their supplies and returned to their car, both men rejuvenated by their acquisitions. Despite the lack of immediate answers, they felt better prepared for whatever came next.

They drove back to Helmworth in silence. Disentangling their minds from the burden they'd both accepted was proving increasingly challenging. It didn't help that the path ahead was so uncharted. But they had fresh supplies and, with them, renewed ambition to solve the enigma of Ry-Lan and his puzzling machine.

* * *

After their trip to Darlington, Alex and Brian decided to stop by Alex's home to sort out their purchases and grab a bite to eat. Entering the kitchen, Alex quickly cleared the table, making space for the gear they had bought. The significance of their discussions and plans still hung in the air, the urgency, for a moment, left unspoken.

As they arranged the various items on the table, Brian looked over at Alex. "You know, if we time it right, we could actually witness Ry-Lan arriving in the car park. We might even understand his actions better this time around," he suggested, his tone expressing optimism.

Alex scanned the equipment. "And we'll be better prepared to handle whatever happened with Ian. We need to see everything first-hand to really understand the dynamics of that encounter."

Brian paused, arranging a mini toolkit next to the first aid kit. "I'll try to nail down the exact timings of Ry-Lan's appearances. If we know when he's going to show up, we can set up discreetly and observe everything without interfering."

The kitchen, usually a place of casual meals and light conversations, now felt like a strategic command centre. Alex passed Brian the water purification tablets, which Brian checked off on their inventory list. "We should consider getting those hidden cameras you mentioned, too," Alex added, "it might give us an extra set of eyes in case we miss anything in real time."

"Yes, we need to remember them," Brian agreed, marking the suggestion on a notepad. "Every detail counts. We can't afford to overlook anything."

As they continued to unpack and organise, the small kitchen was transformed by their enthusiasm and readiness. Each item was carefully checked and placed in order, matching the seriousness of their upcoming mission. The simple act of preparing their equipment reinforced their commitment to understanding the mysterious events surrounding the machine and Ry-Lan.

Their meal, quickly prepared and eaten amid discussions of logistics and strategy, was a brief respite in their intense preparations. As they cleared the table afterwards, both knew the road ahead would be challenging yet potentially revelatory.

"We need a clear plan," Brian said decisively. "Let's start with setting up some observation points around the car park. We'll need to be discreet so we don't draw attention on match day."

"We'll also need to coordinate our arrival," Alex said, tapping a pen against the table. "We can't show up together. It'll look suspicious. I'll get there early and blend in with the crowd. You come a bit later and set up our observation points."

Brian agreed, adding his notes to the map. "I'll keep a low profile. Once everything is in place, I'll join you in the crowd."

The next step was to review their emergency protocols. If anything went wrong, they needed a clear exit strategy. They discussed different scenarios, trying to prepare for any outcome.

As they finished their preparations, Alex sat back in his chair, his expression pensive. "This could be our best chance to understand what's happening. We need to stay sharp and be ready for anything."

Brian shared the same resolve. "We'll be ready. Whatever happens, we'll face it together."

A quiet determination settled over them. The match day against Moseley was not just a sporting event but potentially a key moment in their investigation. But the reality of waiting nearly two weeks was daunting.

"What do we do in the meantime?" Brian asked, breaking the silence. "We can't just sit around for two weeks. There must be something productive we can do."

Alex scratched an ear and nodded at Brian. "We should continue our research. There might be clues we've missed or connections we haven't made yet. We can look into the area's history to see if there's been anything similar in the past."

Brian agreed. "And we can test our equipment. If there's another jump, we need to be ready to handle it. We can run drills and make sure everything is in working order."

"Good idea," Alex said. "We also need to keep an eye out for Ian. He might be the key to all this. If we can find out more about him, it could give us the answers we're looking for."

Chapter 12

Alex got up to adjust the kitchen blind, trying to block the light that, while a welcome change from the recent rain, was now glaring right into their eyes.

"We need to be cautious," Alex began as he returned to his seat. "We can't afford any more mistakes like the last jump."

Brian agreed. "Absolutely. We need to be better prepared. There's no room for errors, especially now that we know how difficult the destination can be to predict."

"First things first," Alex continued, "we need to go back to Bingley farm this afternoon so you can get your car. Plus, you mentioned about collecting more data from the machine's logs."

Brian agreed. "Yes, the jump logs are crucial. They'll help us understand the previous jumps and might give us clues about where and when the machine has been."

"And while we're there," Alex added, "we should talk to Tommy about setting up some kind of barrier around the machine. He doesn't want attention, so he should be willing to help keep it secure."

Brian liked the practicality of Alex's plan. "It's a good idea. If we can keep the machine safe and undisturbed, we'll have more time to study it and prepare for our next moves."

"Alright, let's head to the farm," Alex said finally. "The sooner we start gathering the data, the better."

Brian stood up, stretching his stiff muscles. "Agreed. Let's get moving, Alex."

* * *

Alex and Brian drove to Bingley farm, both lost in reflection as they approached the familiar property. Brian focused on retrieving the valuable jump logs, while Alex was preoccupied with ensuring the machine's security and considering their next moves.

Upon arriving at the farm, Alex parked the car, and they both stepped out, the familiar sight of Tommy's property reigniting their motivation. Tommy was outside, working on some equipment near the barn. Alex waved to him as they approached.

"Hey, Tommy!" Alex called out. "Good to see you. Can I ask a favour, please?"

Tommy looked up, wiping his hands on a rag. "What's up, Alex?"

"We're concerned about keeping the machine safe," Alex began. "We know you don't want too much attention drawn to the site and were wondering if you could set up some kind of barrier around it. Maybe some temporary fencing or something to keep people away."

Tommy seemed keen. "Sure. I can do that. Last thing I want is folks wandering around here causing trouble."

"Thanks, Tommy," Alex said, grateful. "We appreciate it."

While Tommy gathered materials to start setting up the barrier, Brian headed towards the machine, equipped with a notebook, pen, and phone. Using the card, he opened the hatch, got in, and sat down. He began accessing the machine's interface, carefully reviewing the jump logs. Alex joined him, peering over his shoulder as Brian noted the details by hand and took photographs of the screens.

"This is interesting," Brian said, pointing at the screen. "It's fairly easy to get the data from the previous jumps. Some of these coordinates might help us reveal the machine's previous destinations."

"Sure. Take your time. Let's ensure we have all the data we need before leaving."

As Brian continued documenting the logs, Alex considered their situation. The machine had brought them so many more questions than answers, but just maybe, they were on the verge of a groundbreaking discovery. They were in sight of uncovering something significant, and the risks so far seemed worth it.

While Brian worked diligently, Alex joined Tommy, who had already started setting up a temporary fence around the machine. Alex grabbed some posts and helped secure them into the ground while Tommy stretched some rope around the perimeter. The work was straightforward but tiring.

"This should be a good start," Tommy said, admiring their work. "I'll finish it up later."

"Thanks, Tommy," Alex said sincerely. "This is a huge help."

Alex went back to find out how Brian was progressing. "Brian, do you fancy a break?" He indicated that they could sit in his vehicle for a drink. Brian nodded, sat beside him, and took his flask out of his bag.

* * *

The change of location provided a comfortable setting as they sorted through their notes and plans. Brian began examining the data from the jumps he had logged, paying particular attention to the dates.

"They really are intriguing," Brian said, tapping a page in his notebook. "We might be able to find patterns or significant events tied to these dates."

Alex listened, his thoughts drifting to his own personal mission. "Brian, there's something I need to talk to you about," he said, breaking the silence.

Brian looked up from his notes, curious, his gaze lingering. "What is it?" He frowned. "Is it about your brother?"

"Yes. I've been thinking a lot about him," Alex began, his voice tinged with emotion. "As I probably said before ... since it appears that we can travel back in time, I want to go back to try to prevent him from going missing. I was thinking that if I can go back two years to the time before he vanished, maybe I can change things or at least find out what happened to him."

Brian frowned, frustrated with Alex for raising this again right now. "You told me he disappeared in a war zone. Like I've said, I think it's risky, Alex. The Middle East is a volatile place, and there's no telling what might happen."

"I know," Alex replied, "but I have to try. I can't just sit here doing nothing while I believe that I have a chance to save him."

Brian sighed, rubbing his temples. "I understand why you want to do this, but we need to be smart about it. Since traveling to the Middle East is highly dangerous, how about a compromise? You could travel back in time to the farm and then travel conventionally to see Mark."

Alex saw the sense in Brian's suggestion. "You're right. It would be safer that way. What do you think I'd need to take along? "

Brian was put on the spot, but he did his best. "You should take your passport, just in case. And it'd be good to have plenty of cash on hand. As for other things, you can probably get most of what you need after you arrive. Oh, and you'll probably want to take a raincoat to allow for the weather when you arrive."

"I'll need to calculate the coordinates for the jump also," Brian continued. "I think I can work out the time component easily enough. And then we merge it with the location here to take you to the right place."

As Brian got out of the car, Alex called after him. "I appreciate your help, mate. I couldn't do this without you."

Brian gave a smile, though it didn't reach his eyes. Alex suspected that his plan to assist his brother had struck a nerve. "We'll figure this out together, Alex. Let's get some rest and tackle this with fresh eyes tomorrow."

Chapter 13

Sun 7th April 2024

The next morning, Brian was at home, sitting in his study with his laptop open. The house was still, with only the occasional murmur of family life drifting in from the other rooms, until his wife Emily came in and perched on his desk.

"So, how is this secretive task you're involved in progressing?" Emily traced a finger across his brow, "I'm sure you've a couple of furrows that weren't there before."

Brian smiled wryly. "You know I can't answer that. But don't worry ... I'm in no danger." His smile slipped as he saw his wife's expression. "Okay, what's up? You could have asked me that out in the open. Is it Danny?"

"That's very astute." Her expression brightened a little with her remark but soon faded. Running her index finger along his desk, she said, "I've noticed a downturn in his mood lately, and if I'm not mistaken, you have, too. Anyway, I did a bit of prying; his form teacher tells me his work has dropped from its usual standard, but whatever it is, he's keeping quiet about it, both to the teacher and us."

Brian nodded. "You're right. I have noticed it, too. We need to sit down with Danny and persuade him to open up. Just before school probably isn't the best time, though. We'll pick a quiet moment when he's relaxed, okay?"

"Okay." Emily placed a hand on his shoulder. "And as I keep saying, be careful."

Domestic problems apart, Brian felt ready for today's mission, his task being to ensure the coordinates were correct for Alex's upcoming jump. The concept was straightforward, but he was still nervous. It wasn't just about math; that was relatively simple, but a lot was resting on it. As he tapped the keyboard, Brian mused on the implications of sending Alex back, not just for Alex, but for the timeline itself. Could small changes ripple into unintended consequences?

He went into the kitchen and made another cup of coffee, pondering it all. Doubts lingered—had he accounted for all the factors? Time travel was uncharted territory, something he'd thought impossible until just a few days ago.

After reviewing his work, he felt confident enough, yet he decided to triple-check everything before sharing it with Alex. He was due to meet Alex in an hour at the farm, armed with data and a resolve to ensure absolute accuracy. This wasn't solely about scientific curiosity but a friend's desperate hope to alter his past. Before leaving, he spent a few moments with his family, their presence a comforting anchor against the daunting scope of his morning's work.

* * *

The morning air was crisp as Alex arrived at Bingley farm, parking his car as close as he could get to the machine and beside the newly erected barrier that Tommy had put in place. He'd barely stepped out of his car before his phone buzzed, a glance at the caller's identity rapidly souring his mood. Trying to camouflage his frustration, Alex answered lightly, "Yes, CI West?"

"Sergeant Harper," the CI's voice was frosty, not a good sign. "I recall asking you to update me on the incident at Bingley farm, but I cannot recall you giving me one."

Great, Alex thought, sarcasm as well as the icy tone. The CI wasn't happy, but then, she seldom was these days. Keeping away from the tricky subject of the machine as much as possible, Alex replied, "My apologies, Ma'am, but the subject's condition is stable, and he's being closely monitored by the hospital, so there's no change to report. His details remain as yet undetermined."

A sigh from the chief inspector. "And this unidentified object?"

Alex rubbed his eyes, scrambling for the best way to fob her off. 'Well, it's on private property, Ma'am, as you know, and appears quite harmless, and farmer Thompson is happy enough to let it remain on his field for the time being."

"This sounds like a prank to me that's gone wrong." Alex could hear the CI's pen tapping on her desk. "Nonetheless, when I ask for updates, I expect to receive them sooner rather than later. Otherwise, I'm inclined to suspect you're holding something back." And with that ominous comment, CI West cut the call.

Alex walked on, pausing and admiring the sturdy construction before carefully climbing under it to access the machine area. Brian arrived moments later, marked by the squelch of mud underfoot as he made his way to Alex.

Brian had made some notes to go through with Alex. "The most important thing," he started, ensuring Alex was attentive, "is to avoid any interaction with your past self. The potential for unknown consequences is something we just cannot risk."

After a covert glance to ensure his words had sunk in, he continued, "And assuming that you can get in touch with Mark, it's imperative you relay these same warnings. Whatever he does differently based on what you tell him could ripple through time with unforeseen consequences."

Brian's next point focused on Tommy and the farm, emphasizing Alex's unique challenge. "You'll also need to find Tommy and talk to him. He won't realise that you're from the future. You'll need to relay enough info to convince him not to report the machine to the police. We already know that's what he would likely do if he sees it. Hopefully, you'll be gone again before he asks too many questions."

* * *

With all preparations in place, Brian ran through some final checks with Alex. He carefully fitted the bodycam, ensuring it was secure and operational. "As you know, this will record everything you see," Brian reminded him. Also, make sure to use the machine's external cameras before you exit. They'll give you a good view of your surroundings without exposing you prematurely."

After reviewing the settings, Brian proceeded to program the machine. He input the coordinates for the intended time and location, methodically verifying each digit. Alex watched, anticipation and anxiety visible on his features.

Once satisfied, Brian stepped back, remaining outside the machine. "All set. Remember, keep a low profile and avoid unnecessary interactions," he reminded Alex, his voice serious but supportive.

Alex breathed deeply as he settled into the machine's operator seat. He felt the familiar hum of the machine powering up, the console lighting up with a soft glow. Brian gave him a final thumbs-up, signalling readiness, and stepped away to monitor from a safe distance. As the machine began its sequence, the reality of his journey into the past solidified, and with a quiet determination, Alex prepared to face whatever awaited him in the undetermined timeline he was about to enter.

Thu 7th April 2022

Alex braced for the familiar sensations as he activated the jump sequence, expecting the pastoral greens of Bingley farm to reappear once he opened the hatch. Instead, as he unfastened his seat restraint, a novel sensation seized him—an unsettling lightness, an absence of down that defied his every expectation. Weightlessness enveloped him, a profound silence pervading the cabin as the sudden realisation dawned on him: he was not where he was supposed to be.

Struggling against the zero-gravity environment, Alex reached out, flailing for stability as he floated free of his seat. His movements were clumsy and uncoordinated as he propelled himself towards the machine's control panel. Each attempt to press a button propelled him backwards, his efforts to navigate the cabin turning into a desperate ballet in the void.

Determined, Alex managed to navigate to the camera controls, activating the external feeds with a push that sent him tumbling back again. The screens flickered to life, revealing not the expected English countryside but a vista of an entirely different nature. The camera's panoramic view displayed a breathtaking expanse of space, the Milky Way sprawling across the cosmic sea like a celestial tapestry woven from stardust and light.

The beauty of the universe, vast and unfathomable, stretched out before him. Stars twinkled in the infinite darkness, planets and celestial bodies orbiting in the silent choreography of the cosmos. The surreal realisation that he was adrift in the vacuum of space sent a shiver of awe mixed with dread through Alex. This was the grandeur of the universe laid bare, magnificent yet terrifying in its boundless mystery.

Alex's heart pounded in his chest, a frantic metronome amidst the tranquillity of the stars. The isolation was overwhelming, a solitary human presence floating amongst the celestial wonders that humanity had long dreamed of exploring. Yet this dream had turned into a nightmare, the splendour of the galaxy a cold and dangerous backdrop to his growing panic.

Desperation crept in as Alex grappled with the controls, each movement exaggerated by his weightless state. He needed to initiate the return sequence, to escape this beautiful but alien expanse and return to the familiarity of Earth. The machine's interface, designed for terrestrial use, was ill-suited for navigation in zero gravity, its buttons slipping under his fingertips as he struggled to anchor himself.

Time seemed to stretch into eternity as Alex fought against the push and pull of his own movements. The vastness of space, once a realm of dreams and aspirations, now felt like a prison, its bars made not of steel but cosmic distances unfathomable to the human mind.

Chapter 14

In the suffocating silence of the void, Alex's pulse hammered against the chilling coldness of space that enveloped him. Adrift among the stars, the terror of the infinite pressed upon him as he floated weightlessly, a lone speck of humanity unmoored from the earth. With a desperate scramble, he lunged towards the machine's control panel, his movements awkward as each attempt to press a button sent him drifting further away.

Fighting the disorientation of weightlessness, Alex managed to wrap his arm around a support strut, pulling himself back to the panel with a determined grunt. His fingers, trembling with adrenaline, danced across the interface, initiating the return sequence. The familiar hum of the machine gearing up was the most comforting sound he'd ever heard, a promise of a return to the world he belonged in.

Sun 7th April 2024

The transition back to Bingley farm was abrupt, wrenching him from the ethereal calm of space to the grounding force of Earth's gravity. He stumbled out of the machine, the farm's lush green a vivid contrast to the deep black of space he had left behind. The Earth's forces clung to his limbs like chains, making each step feel like wading through deep water.

Alex's breaths came in sharp, ragged gasps as he collapsed onto the grass, vomiting profusely as the farm's familiar smells and sounds swirled around him in a dizzying haze. The ground beneath him was solid and real, yet the echo of the stars lingered in his mind, a haunting reminder of the vastness he had just escaped.

The sky above Bingley farm seemed impossibly high as he lay there, a thin veil separating him from the void he had narrowly escaped. His heart continued to race, pounding out the rhythm of a man who had touched the cosmos and returned—shaken but alive.

* * *

As Alex lay sprawled on the grass, each gasp for air slicing through the quiet of the farm, Brian rushed to his side, concern and urgency deeply visible across his face. Dropping to his knees beside Alex, he supported him gently, guiding him to sit up while murmuring words meant to soothe, though his own voice trembled with the undercurrent of alarm.

"Easy, Alex. Just take it slow," Brian coaxed, his hands steady on Alex's shoulders as he scanned his friend's face for signs of injury or distress.

The world slowly stopped spinning for Alex. He relied on Brian's support, his shaking limbs and pale complexion giving evidence of his ordeal. Gathering the shards of his composure, he locked eyes with Brian, the vast emptiness of space still reflecting in his gaze. "Brian ... I didn't come back here," Alex's voice broke as he spoke, the words almost catching in his throat, "I was in space, floating among the stars."

Brian's face showed his confusion and worry. "Space? But how—" His voice trailed off as the implications of Alex's unintended journey began to dawn on him, muddling his scientific mind with too many unanswered questions.

"I don't know," Alex replied, his breathing starting to even out as he clung to the grounding presence of his friend. "Everything was set for two years back, not ... not out there." He gestured vaguely upwards towards the heavens that had so briefly been his prison.

They sat silently for a moment, the soft rustle of the farm's foliage swaying in a gentle breeze, providing a peaceful backdrop to the chaos of emotions swirling between them. Brian raced through the calculations and coordinates, trying to pinpoint the anomaly that had sent his friend hurtling through the cosmic void instead of back through time.

Finally, with a steadying breath, Alex stood, supported by Brian's firm grip. "We need to check the logs, see what went wrong," he stated, the resolve in his voice masking the residual fear that lingered at the edge of his thoughts.

Brian nodded, the scientist in him already pivoting towards solving the puzzle. "Let's go back to the machine. We'll go through everything, step by step."

Together, they walked back to the enigmatic sphere that sat silently in the field, its secrets yet unspooled, its threat subdued again but as potent as ever.

* * *

With scepticism and dread, Brian climbed into the machine that had just returned from an unexpected odyssey. The interior still held a chill, a silent testament to the cold void it had traversed. As he settled in front of the control panel, his fingers danced over the buttons with practiced ease, calling up the video feed from the onboard cameras.

The screen flickered to life, displaying the footage that Alex had experienced first-hand. The images were breathtaking and terrifying in equal measure: a panorama of stars scattered across the infinite black canvas of space, the Milky Way arcing through it like a celestial river. It was a view that humankind had seen only through the lenses of telescopes and spacecraft, now vividly displayed on the screen of a machine meant to traverse time, not the vast reaches of space.

Brian's eyes widened as he took in the sight, his scientific mind grappling with the implications. The footage was irrefutable. Alex hadn't hallucinated; the coordinates had somehow catapulted him into the vacuum of space. "This ... this is incredible," Brian murmured under his breath, awe mingling with a tinge of fear. "But how ..."

He replayed the footage, noting the positions of stars and celestial landmarks, trying to glean any clue that might explain how their calculations had gone so astonishingly awry. With each pass, the reality of their miscalculation sank deeper. There was no denying the evidence in front of him. The machine, their prized anomaly, had defied not just their expectations but the very laws they believed governed it.

"I made a mistake," Brian finally conceded, his voice conveying defeat and perplexity. "Or we've fundamentally misunderstood something about the machine's operation. It's not just navigating through time but space as well ... and we don't fully understand how or why."

Brian felt the significance of the revelation within the cramped confines of the machine. He stepped out, his mind buzzing with equations and theories that needed revising or perhaps rethinking from the ground up. He met Alex's expectant gaze, his own filled with a cautious determination.

"We need to review everything, every calculation, every assumption we've made about how this machine works. We're missing a piece of the puzzle, and it's a dangerous one," Brian stated, resolved to unravel the mystery that had nearly cost his friend his life.

Together, they would explore the science behind the machine further, both daunted and driven by the new frontier that had just unfolded before them.

* * *

As the implications of their recent ordeal settled in, a deep, unnerving fear gripped Alex and Brian. The quiet of the field stood in opposition to the turmoil brewing within them as they confronted the reality of their discovery. The machine, their bridge across time, had revealed its potential to thrust its passenger anywhere—across the vast, cold expanses of space itself.

Brian paced slowly while his thoughts raced. "I've made too many assumptions with the mathematics of it all," he admitted, his voice tinged with regret and a newfound respect for the forces they were tampering with. "The power of this machine is just staggering! But it's also dangerous."

He paused, turning to face Alex, his expression grave. "I'm kicking myself, because there's something else I've just realised," Brian continued. "I should have known it would fail because if you were actually going to travel back and speak to Tommy two years ago ... he already would have known about the machine well before Ry-Lan's arrival."

Still shaken from his ordeal, Alex leaned against the wall, absorbing Brian's words. The puzzle pieces were slowly forming a picture that neither of them had anticipated. "So, you're saying Tommy's reaction to the machine appearing four days ago ... It would have been different. He would have recognised it, known what it was."

"Exactly." Brian became solemn. "This means that either our understanding of how to direct the jumps is flawed, or each jump might create a different ... timeline or reality. We might not just be crossing through time but splintering it, creating or moving through alternatives we don't yet understand."

The weight of their actions, the potential consequences, hung between them heavier than the Earth's gravity that had so recently eluded Alex. The terror of the unknown – powers not meant to be meddled with by human hands – overshadowed the thrill of scientific discovery.

Their reflection was not just on the scientific implications but also the moral and existential ones. Could they, should they continue using the machine? The question loomed large, the answer as elusive and fraught with danger as the stars that now haunted Alex's memory.

They both knew that caution would guide their every step forward almost without needing to speak aloud. The adventure, the exploration they had embarked on, had shown them the wonders of the universe and its terrifying vastness and indifference.

* * *

Brian glanced at the machine, then back at Alex, his face lined with concern. "We should hold off for now," he suggested, his tone measured and authoritative. "Today has shown us just how dangerous this all is. We need to understand more before we use the machine again."

Still grappling with the aftermath of his harrowing experience, Alex felt disappointed but knew the wisdom in Brian's words. He understood, having already reached the same conclusion. "You're right," Alex agreed slowly, his gaze drifting towards the silent machine that had promised so much adventure. "We should stop using the machine until we understand what went wrong."

"We'll document as much as we can," Brian proposed, a spark of determination lighting his features. "I think I can probably get there by studying the navigation history in greater detail. It's the only way we can safely move forward."

The plan reassured Alex. "And there's still a wealth of data to analyse. We haven't exhausted what the machine can teach us. Not by a long way."

This conclusion, born from a blend of caution and respect for the unknown, marked a hiatus in their direct interactions with the machine. For now, it would remain an object of study rather than a vehicle to the past or future. They continued their diligent work under the morning sun, surrounded by the quiet of the farm.

Alex also had work to do. He decided to continue looking into Ian Cooper, postponing any further enquiries until his return to work on Monday. The situation called for patience and tact, particularly since he realised that his superiors, especially CI West, would soon scrutinize his work.

There was also a future visit to the stadium to prepare for. They wanted to be ready for Ry-Lan's expected reappearance. They planned to methodically scout the location better at the point of his coming to understand and anticipate the phenomena associated with the machine's operation.

Their agreement to proceed with caution and diligence formed the backbone of their strategy, combining Brian's analytical prowess with Alex's pragmatic approach to fieldwork. As they left the farm, their morning's resolve transformed into a concerted commitment to explore the machine's secrets, guided by a balanced approach of scientific enquiry and operational prudence.

* * *

As Alex drove home, his mind churned with concerns about his brother Mark, whose fate remained a tormenting enigma. The unsuccessful jump not only underscored the dangers of their task but also the immense difficulties in interacting with the past. This whirlpool of thoughts impelled Alex to reach out to Kate, Mark's wife, in a desperate attempt to reconnect and perhaps find another way to aid his brother.

Upon arriving home, Alex made the call, his heart pounding. When Kate answered, her voice was cold and distant.

"Kate, it's Alex. I just wanted to talk about Mark. I need to know if there's anything I can do to help," Alex began, trying to keep his tone gentle.

"There's nothing you can do, Alex. You've done enough already," Kate replied curtly.

"Please, Kate, what have I done? I just want to help," Alex pleaded.

"Help? You think you can help? " Kate's voice was laced with bitterness.

"Kate, I ..." Alex struggled for words, but before he could continue, she hung up.

Alex stood there, phone in hand, feeling anger and helplessness wash over him. Kate's abrupt dismissal felt like yet another door slamming shut on him, leaving him isolated with his worries. Just why was Kate so resentful of him? He shook his head, the answer to that one he could not fathom.

The frustration of the day, compounded by this personal rejection, made the challenges ahead seem even more daunting. As he put his phone back in his pocket, the quiet of his house seemed to amplify the uncertainty and solitude that lay before him, a reminder of the complex path that still awaited him and Brian.

Chapter 15

<u>Mon 8th April 2024 +</u>

Time had passed since the harrowing experience in space, but the memories lingered, casting a shadow over Alex's daily routine. The relentless thrum of police work offered little distraction. He moved through his shifts at the station, mechanically handling cases and reports, yet his mind was elsewhere, replaying the weightlessness, the vastness, the silent expanse.

The investigation into Ian Cooper provided no solace either. Alex had hoped for some breakthrough, a hidden connection to illuminate their path. Instead, Ian's life was depressingly ordinary. A secondary school teacher with a minor caution for marijuana possession, Ian's record was basically clean, his actions unremarkable. Alex combed through his employment record, spoke to his headmaster, and even scrutinised Ian's social media, but found nothing of substance. The man was a nobody, living a life devoid of any apparent ties to the extraordinary events Alex was investigating.

Meanwhile, Brian immersed himself in the machine's logs. Just as Alex's world was marked by unrelenting frustration, Brian's was filled with methodical enquiry. Each line of data was a puzzle piece, each entry a potential clue. He spent hours in front of his computer, cross-referencing logs, plotting coordinates, and mapping the machine's destinations. Brian's academic rigour was his refuge and weapon against the unknowable chaos the machine represented. He was determined to uncover a pattern, a logic to the jumps that had thus far eluded them.

For Alex, the nighttime was the hardest. He would lie awake, staring at the ceiling, his mind a whirlpool of questions and regrets. He thought of Mark often, his brother's fate entwined with his own unresolved guilt. The call to Mark's wife, Kate, still echoed in his mind as a reminder of his failure to connect. He had hoped for some connection, some bridge back to his brother, but the hostility he encountered left him feeling more isolated than ever.

Brian, too, felt the burden of their shared responsibilities. He was concerned for Alex and the emotional and psychological toll the recent events took on him. Their renewed partnership, forged in the crucible of shared discovery, was their most significant asset as they navigated this uncertain journey.

As time passed, the sense of urgency that had initially driven them began to wane, replaced by a grim determination. They were in uncharted territory, guided only by their intellect and resolve. Alex's thoughts kept drifting back to the machine, to the infinite possibilities and the dangers it held. The sense of being on the cusp of something monumental was both thrilling and terrifying.

Despite the setbacks and mounting pressure, they had an unspoken agreement: they would continue. With all its mysteries and risks, the machine was their only hope of finding answers, of understanding who Ry-Lan was and what had happened to him, and of possibly even altering the course of their own lives. They just needed to proceed with caution, patience, and an unwavering commitment to the truth.

Sat 13th April 2024

Late Saturday evening, Alex's phone rang as he prepared for bed. The name on the screen—Brian—made his pulse quicken. Hastening to answer, he nearly knocked over a cold cup of coffee.

"Hey Brian, what have you got?" Alex enquired, his curiosity obvious.

"Alex, I think I've got it," Brian said, his voice exuding excitement and exhaustion. "I know what went wrong with the last jump. I've meticulously plotted the jump logs, comparing them against astronomical data. When I rendered the coordinates in a 3D computer model, it became obvious."

Alex was intrigued. "What did you find?"

"You know how we tried to send you back to the same location, but two years ago?"

"Yes, and I ended up in space," Alex replied.

"Well, that's because the Earth had moved. It wasn't in the same place two years ago. The Earth is constantly moving. It rotates around the sun."

"And?"

"I just didn't it think through properly. We used the same location from where we were and merged it with the date from two years ago. In one respect, we were lucky. The Earth doesn't travel around the sun in exactly one year. It actually takes 365 days plus a quarter. Fortunately, the coordinate system already compensates for the leap year. It uses a kind of 'universal time' format."

"Go on."

"So, you would think the Earth would be in the same place two solar years earlier. But I had forgotten that the solar system is also rotating around the centre of the galaxy!"

"OK. I guess it sounds obvious now that you say it. How did you figure it out?"

"When I plotted the points on a three-dimensional chart," Brian explained. "I could see the pattern. The points formed a circular path, just as the Earth rotates around the sun."

"A circular path?" Alex's interest grew as he visualised the data in his mind.

"Exactly," Brian continued, "but there's more to it. Over time, these coordinates develop into a spiral pattern—a corkscrew. It's also showing our solar system's movement through the galaxy."

Alex processed this, the implications dawning on him slowly. "So, you're saying the machine's coordinates change according to where the Earth is in space, too?"

"Precisely," Brian confirmed, his voice gaining a shade more confidence.

"That's incredible," Alex replied, a touch of awe creeping into his voice. "But what does this mean for us? Does it give us more control over the jumps?"

"It's very complicated," Brian admitted. "While I believe I can now calculate the time of a jump accurately, determining the location is still beyond me. There are too many variables. I would struggle to calculate where the Earth is at any point in time, let alone where any particular place on Earth would be. We're talking about calculating precise movements on a cosmic scale."

Alex sighed. He was pleased that Brian had made such progress, but also disappointed that Brian could not calculate the trip he wanted.

Alex had an idea. "Brian, what if you publish your findings? You could claim the discovery of a new method for charting space over time. Just don't mention the machine. It could be a significant breakthrough for you."

Brian's hesitated. "Publish the data? Alex, haven't you considered the potential ramifications? What if doing that would alter the future? What if it changes the sequence of events leading to the creation of the jump machine itself?"

Alex frowned, the enormity of Brian's concerns sinking in. "I get your point, but isn't this too big to just sit on? We're sitting on something really special here. It could revolutionise the way we understand our place in the galaxy."

"But at what cost?" Brian countered, frustration creeping into his voice. "Any interference—publications, announcements—could ripple through time in ways we can't predict. We are dealing with forces we barely understand."

Alex sighed, running a hand through his hair as he stared blankly at the disorganised papers scattered across his desk. The implications were staggering, and the more he thought about it, the more overwhelmed he felt. "I know you're right, but it feels like there is so much potential here."

Silence stretched between them, burdened by the importance of their moral dilemma. Brian finally broke it with a softer, more contemplative tone. "This is bigger than just the science, Alex. It's about understanding our responsibility. We're not just dealing with abstract concepts; we're tinkering with the fabric of reality."

Alex swallowed hard, feeling uncharacteristic vulnerability. "I feel like we've opened a Pandora's box, and now, we're scrambling to understand what we've unleashed."

A lighter silence followed this admission, one filled with the unspoken recognition of their shared load. After a moment, Brian shifted the conversation. "On a different note, how is Ry-Lan doing? Any progress there?"

Alex shook his head, even though Brian couldn't see him. "Not much to report. Ry-Lan is stable, but we're not seeing any major breakthroughs. I looked into Ian but found nothing useful. I've done my best to investigate him, but I can't see anything that links him to the machine. Not yet, at least."

"That's a shame," Brian sighed. "It seems like every step forward is matched by two steps back. It feels like we're trying to solve a jigsaw puzzle without having all the pieces."

"Exactly," Alex agreed, his voice betraying exhaustion. "It's a lot to manage. And now, with these new findings, it's like the puzzle just expanded into another dimension."

"Maybe it's not all bad," Brian suggested. "We've made significant progress. We've got a lead on the jumps, even if it's just 'when' and not 'where.' Sometimes, the path isn't clear until you're halfway down it."

Alex drew a deep breath, allowing himself a momentary glimmer of hope. "Yeah, maybe. It's hard to see the bigger picture when we're mired in the daily grind. But you're right. At least we have something to hold onto."

"We'll get there," Brian affirmed, resolve returning to his voice. "We've come this far, haven't we? All we need is time. Which, ironically, we might have more control over than we think."

The corners of Alex's mouth lifted into a small smile. "Time. Funny how it's both our greatest asset and our toughest challenge."

The conversation shifted again. Alex knew they couldn't afford to sit idle, waiting for answers to materialise. The upcoming rugby match at Mowden Park stadium loomed in his mind—a crucial opportunity to gather more data and potentially witness Ry-Lan's next appearance.

"Brian, we need to be proactive about this," Alex said, breaking the contemplative silence. "What if we went to the rugby match at Mowden Park? We know that Ry-Lan's expected to appear there, so we might gain some insights into the machine's operations."

Brian considered the suggestion. "It makes sense," he finally said. "But we have to approach this with utmost caution. One wrong move, and we could influence things in ways we can't foresee."

Alex nodded, even though it was a gesture lost over the phone. "I agree. We'll need to be discreet and keep our distance. But it could really help us to understand what is going on."

"Absolutely," Brian agreed. "But let's be clear about one thing: our primary goal is observation. We're not there to interact or intervene unless it's absolutely necessary. We don't fully understand the implications of our presence, and we need to tread lightly."

"Understood," Alex affirmed. "We'll need to work out the timings and make sure we're there well ahead of Ry-Lan. And, of course, Ian, too. The less rushed we are, the more control we'll have over the situation."

Brian's voice took on a note of determination. "Then it's settled. We'll attend the match and gather whatever data we can. And we'll remain vigilant. This could very well be our best chance to understand more about why Ry-Lan came here and how we can help him."

"Got it," Alex replied. "We've got a lot riding on this. Let's make sure we're ready for whatever comes our way."

As they ended the call, Alex felt excited and knew it would now affect his sleep. The upcoming visit to Mowden Park was full of unknowns, though it could well be the key to unlocking more of the machine's mysteries. They were stepping into unknown territory, but at least they were taking that step together, armed with caution, discretion, and a determination to unearth the truth.

Mon 15th April 2024

The following week arrived without ceremony, and Alex began his usual tour of his patch. Trying to stay busy, Alex decided to pop in to see Tommy at the farm, with maybe a quick glimpse at the machine to check it was OK. Driving down the familiar dirt road, he felt a sense of normality creeping in, one that juxtaposed awkwardly with the extraordinary circumstances he was embroiled in.

When he arrived, the farm was unusually quiet. The usual clatter of work and animal sounds were conspicuously absent. Surprised, Alex approached the farmhouse and knocked on the door, but there was no answer. He wandered around the property for a few minutes, expecting Tommy to appear any moment.

After wandering around the farm for a while and finding no sign of Tommy, Alex took out his phone and called him. He paced back and forth as the phone rang with mounting impatience. Just when he was about to hang up, Tommy answered.

"Alex, hey! What's up?" Tommy sounded cheerful but slightly out of breath.

"Hey, Tommy. I decided to pop by your place to see you, but you're nowhere to be found. I just wanted to check you're OK," Alex said, glancing around the empty farm.

"Ah, I'm sorry about that. I didn't know you were coming," Tommy replied, his tone becoming a bit more serious. "I'm over at Greenfell's. Some of John's sheep have taken ill, and he needed an extra pair of hands to help out."

"That sounds ominous," Alex replied, feeling a pang of unease. "Do you need any help?"

"No, we've got it under control for now, but thanks for the offer. It's gonna be one of those weeks. I can feel it," Tommy explained.

"Alright, just let me know if you need anything," Alex said, ending the call with a promise to catch up again soon. It was rare for Tommy to be away from the farm, and the unusualness of the situation added to Alex's growing sense of unease.

With some spare time, Alex decided to visit the hospital to check on Ry-Lan. As he entered Ry-Lan's room, the sight of the motionless figure and the monitors displaying steady vitals greeted him. A nurse he'd not met before was examining one of the monitors.

"Hello," Alex said, stepping closer. "I'm Sergeant Harper. I've been checking in on Ry-Lan regularly. Has there been any change in his condition?"

The nurse turned, offering a polite smile. "Hello, Sergeant. I'm Claire. No, unfortunately, there hasn't been any significant change. His condition remains stable, but we're not seeing any signs of consciousness."

Alex sighed. "It's been days. Is there anything more we can do?"

Claire shook her head gently. "We're doing everything we can. Sometimes, it just takes time. All we can do is monitor and hope for the best. It's unusual, I admit, but we're still running various tests."

"Thank you, Claire. I appreciate all you and the team are doing," Alex said, understanding the complexity yet feeling helpless.

After Claire left the room, Alex sat by Ry-Lan's bedside for a few minutes, his mind churning with questions and uncertainties. The enigmatic figure remained motionless, representing the mysteries they were trying to unravel. But despite the lack of progress, Alex felt determined. If there was any chance to uncover more about the machine and Ry-Lan's connection to it, they had to take it.

Returning to his car, Alex felt the stress of his upcoming mission at Mowden Park settling heavily on his shoulders. The visit to the farm and the hospital hadn't brought any new revelations, but it had focused his resolve. They were standing on the edge of something monumental, and every step had to be taken with the utmost caution.

Later that evening, Alex and Brian spoke again to finalise their plans for the rugby match. As they would be coming from different directions, they decided to travel separately and park and meet in the stadium car park.

Both men knew the significance of the upcoming events at Mowden Park. The coming weekend held the potential for a significant breakthrough or perhaps a missed opportunity. It may all come down to a slim time window and they needed to get it right.

Chapter 16

<u>Sat 20th April 2024</u>

The day of the rugby match at Mowden Park Stadium finally arrived. As Alex pulled into the car park, he could see Brian already waiting for him in his car. Alex parked close by and went over to speak to him.

"Hey, Brian," Alex called to him.

Brian left his car to greet Alex. "Great to see you again, mate."

"I see you found a good spot then," Alex said, motioning towards Brian's car.

"Yes," Brian replied. "I got here early. Are you ready to go?"

They headed towards the stadium entrance, but instead of going inside, Alex and Brian lingered outside, mingling with the arriving fans. They scanned the crowd, examining each new face, firmly focused on trying to spot Ian.

"I feel like a detective tailing a suspect," Brian joked as he surveyed the growing crowd. "Is this what it's like to be you?"

Alex chuckled. "Hardly. Most of the time, it's traffic control and paperwork."

They shifted location every few minutes, trying to cover different vantage points without appearing suspicious. As more and more people arrived, the noise from inside the stadium increased.

"I don't see him yet," Brian said, his voice edged with frustration. "Do you think he'll come?"

"We have to assume he will," Alex replied. "It's our best chance to observe and maybe understand what's about to happen."

As the start of the match drew closer, the crowds around the entrance began thinning out. Alex glanced at his watch. "We should go in. If he's here, then he must be inside already."

Brian agreed, and together they approached the turnstiles. The process of getting inside wasn't as straightforward as they expected. The announcer was reading the line-ups, and the noise made it difficult for them to hear each other.

"Where are our seats again?" Brian shouted, looking slightly disoriented by the noisy crowd.

"Section B, row 12," Alex replied, guiding them through the maze of cheering fans and waving flags.

Reaching their seats involved more squeezing past enthusiastic spectators, each additional "excuse me" and "sorry" feeling like another layer of their disguise being removed. Finally, they settled into their seats, resigned to watching the game and waiting.

As the match kicked off, the crowd's energy surged, an infectious wave doing little to dampen their internal tension. Alex glanced around, still partly expecting Ian to appear out of nowhere but trying to stay inconspicuous.

They occasionally exchanged quiet words, discussing possible sightings among the many people. The crowd's enthusiasm surrounded them like a bubble, making their private tension feel even more amplified.

"Do you have the equipment?" Alex asked quietly, his eyes fixed on the game but his mind far away.

"Yeah," Brian replied, patting his bag casually. "I brought night-vision cameras and a couple of other gadgets. Nothing too obvious."

"Good," Alex said, allowing himself a brief moment of relief. "We'll need to stay sharp. Timing is everything."

The game progressed, punctuated by cheers and shouts from the enthusiastic crowd. Alex and Brian's conversation intermittently returned to their plan, feeling the day's importance with every word. They had mapped out various scenarios prepared for the expected and the unforeseen.

"I still can't believe we're doing this," Brian muttered under his breath during a particularly tense moment in the game.

"Nor can I," Alex agreed, scanning the field's perimeter. "But it's our best shot at understanding more about Ry-Lan and what he's doing. We have to see this through."

Another roar from the crowd signalled a significant play on the field, but Alex and Brian were too absorbed in their conversation to pay much attention. Their thoughts were aligned on the same track, running over details and potential outcomes of the evening.

As the match neared halftime, the reality of their situation started to affect them. The atmosphere in the stadium was electric, but it did little to ease their nerves. They shared a brief look, understanding the significance of the upcoming hours.

Alex sighed, running a hand through his hair. "This waiting game is killing me. I hate not knowing what's next."

Brian gave a reassuring smile. "I know what you mean, but we've got this. At least there is a point in time that we know where Ian and Ry-Lan will be."

Halftime provided another opportunity to scan the crowd. They made their way into the bar area and stood at either end to watch the punters queue up and get served. But still no sign of Ian.

As the second half began, Alex thought of the evening ahead. Would the machine come? Surely, it must. He knew it would. He'd seen it two weeks ago or in a few hours' time. He shook his head and tried to distract himself with the match.

*　*　*

As the final whistle blew and the crowd erupted into cheers, Alex and Brian exchanged glances conveying both relief and heightened anticipation. The match had been a backdrop to their true purpose, and now, as the crowd began to head home, it was time to discuss their next moves.

"Let's grab something to eat. We need to stay sharp for whatever happens next," Alex suggested, already mapping out the immediate future in his mind.

"Agreed," Brian replied, looking around and pulling out his phone. "There's a small shop not far from here. I fancy a walk anyway. Been sitting down all day."

"Alright. I'll stay here and keep a watch from my car. I don't want to lose our spot."

"Perfect," Brian said, checking the directions on his phone. "I'll be quick."

Alex watched as Brian merged with the dispersing crowd and then returned to his vehicle. He settled into the driver's seat, scanning the emptying car park while his mind raced through possible scenarios for the evening.

Minutes later, the first few raindrops spattered against the windshield. Alex glanced up at the sky, now heavy with dark clouds.

He hoped Brian wouldn't be long, knowing the rain would only complicate things.

Brian, phone in hand, walked briskly towards the shop. Even though he had known rain was forecasted for the night, he'd forgotten to bring an umbrella. The rain intensified as he reached the shop, making the short trek feel much longer.

By the time he entered the store, Brian was already regretting his oversight. He grabbed a couple of sandwiches, bottled water, and some crisps, hurrying to the checkout. He remained focused on their mission, the excitement of the match already a distant memory.

With the purchases in hand, Brian stepped back into the steady rain, quickly returning to the car park. The cold, wet drops seeped through his clothing, and he cursed himself silently for not being better prepared. Keeping his head down, he pushed on, determined not to let this small inconvenience disrupt their plans.

When he finally reached Alex's car, he tapped on the window, dripping and somewhat bedraggled. Alex unlocked the door, and Brian slid into the passenger seat, handing over the food.

"You look like a drowned rat," Alex commented, slight amusement breaking through his tension.

Brian shook his head, water droplets flying. "Yeah, yeah. Laugh it up. Let's just eat and get ready. We've still got a long wait ahead."

They ate their sandwiches in reflective silence, Alex casting an occasional sideways glance at Brian. Although with matters relating to the machine, Brian was his usual sharp-minded self, he'd seemed drawn and strained today, and Alex wondered whether something else was bothering him. Of course, the soaking he'd just taken wouldn't have helped, but no, that wasn't it. Alex decided to take the plunge.

"Are you feeling under the weather? Excuse the pun, but you don't seem quite yourself today."

"Huh!" Brian gave a brief chuckle, but his smile soon faded. He sighed and, bunching up the empty sandwich carton and crisp packet ready for disposal said, "Danny's been acting oddly of late. He's not eating properly, his form teacher has noticed a drop in his schoolwork, and whatever's going on with him, he's not telling either Emily or me." Brian looked out at the rainswept panorama. "We're going to have it out with him, diplomatically, of course, most likely tomorrow."

Alex had no children in his ill-fated marriage, but that didn't mean he couldn't sympathise with Brian. "I guess he's approaching that age, Brian, I mean…"

"I know what you mean," Brian cut in, a hand on Alex's shoulder. "Adolescence, we've all been there – I'm not looking forward to our 'little chat', but we'll sort it out, the three of us." Brian promptly switched the conversation back to matters at hand, with the patter of rain on the car roof a constant reminder of their challenges, but it also reinforced their determination. Every moment brought them closer to the evening's crucial events.

Their conversation returned to the details of their plan, and wondering how it would play out. They were acutely aware of the ticking clock, both in terms of the impending event and the broader implications of their actions.

As the rain continued falling, they prepared for whatever the night might bring, their minds sharp and hearts steeled for the unknown, ready to witness a jump from the receiving end and unravel more of the mystery that had drawn them into this extraordinary situation.

* * *

After the quick meal, Alex picked up his binoculars again and scanned the expanse of the nearly deserted car park. The dark tarmac stretched like an unforgiving ocean, punctuated by a few vehicles that seemed aloof, static, and indifferent to the unfolding vigil. They sipped their lukewarm drinks, the sweetness mingling with the edge of their anxiety. The gritty interplay of flavours mirrored the tension in the air.

Time, ever the trickster, crawled with a torturous slowness. Each tangible tick of the clock heightened the anticipation to an almost unbearable pitch. The minutes became heavier, hanging densely in the air, until they seemed to stretch and bend reality around them.

Then, defying both expectation and calculation, the machine appeared unexpectedly at precisely 7:45 p.m. Alex's heart skipped a beat, a startled breath catching in his throat.

Relief washed over them like a cool breeze on a hot summer's day. The machine's presence dissipated the gnawing doubt that had set up camp in the recesses of his mind. Yes, their theories had not led them astray; the mysterious machine was not a figment of their desperate imaginations but a tangible entity, part of the mystery they were set to crack open.

"It's here. And it's early," Alex whispered, the words escaping like a cautious breeze. He exchanged a glance with Brian, whose eyes mirrored awe and trepidation. Both understood the significance of this early arrival—either it implied new patterns or an urgency they hadn't accounted for.

From their vantage point within the car, they watched the sphere with bated breath. It was perfectly still, a silent sentinel that hinted at both vast technological prowess and an eerie sense of purpose. There were no visible seams, no indications of how it functioned. It seemed pulled from a different dimension where such marvels were commonplace.

"What is he doing?" Brian murmured, his eyes never leaving the sphere. "Do you think he's scanning the area?"

"Could be," Alex replied, allowing themselves a moment of fascination. "I hope he doesn't see us."

The car park's ambient sounds—the distant hum of traffic, the occasional chirp of a night bird—seemed to fade away, leaving only the eerie quiet surrounding the machine. Reassured yet on edge, they continued their vigil, noting every detail, every subtle shine and shadow of the spherical enigma before them.

It didn't communicate or move—it simply existed as if waiting for an unknown cue. Yet, in its stillness, it conveyed a multitude of possibilities. Alex's mind raced, weaving through hypotheses and potential outcomes. They had cracked open a new layer of understanding, but the depths of the mystery threatened to plunge them into uncharted territories.

Alex and Brian's hearts pounded in synchrony with the steady hum of anticipation. The early arrival was more than a mere surprise; it served as a reminder that the calm could be deceptive, that layers of secrets lay buried just beneath the surface, waiting to be uncovered. And as they sat there, watching the enigmatic sphere's form against the twilight, one thing was clear: this was only the beginning.

* * *

After what seemed like ages, a panel in the seamless surface of the sphere slid open effortlessly. A shadowed figure emerged from its metallic womb, stepping out with a fluid grace that belied the moment's tension. Alex squinted through the binoculars, heart pounding with excitement and trepidation. The figure was clad in attire remarkably similar to Ry-Lan's, a utilitarian blend of form and function, but it was immediately apparent that this was someone else.

The newcomer moved with a calculated precision, each movement deliberate and measured. He appeared almost spectral against the urban backdrop, a ghost from some forgotten future given solid form. The man's eyes were sharp, scanning the surroundings with methodical thoroughness. He approached the machine, hands caressing its surface with an intimate familiarity.

Alex's focus sharpened as the man's right hand moved with an unnerving exactness, articulating commands in the air like an integrated device. Seeing the specifics from this distance was impossible, but the motion was unmistakable—and unprecedented. The hand seemed to shimmer faintly, tiny, enigmatic pulses of light emanating from beneath the skin, casting small but significant glows onto his face.

"He's controlling something," Brian whispered, eyes wide with awe and trepidation.

"Or communicating," Alex replied, his voice low and tense. The possibilities were endless, each more unsettling than the last.

The figure then turned abruptly and began jogging towards the main road. His pace was brisk, every stride suggesting a purposeful energy. The movement was almost rhythmic, evidencing his physical fitness. His jog had a resolve, as though he was on a mission that warranted no delay.

"What do you think he's doing?" Brian murmured, half to himself.

Alex didn't answer immediately, scrambling to piece together the fragments of this unfolding enigma. They watched in breathless silence as the man's form receded into the growing dusk, becoming a silhouette against the encroaching night and ultimately dissolving into the urban surroundings.

The machine remained inert, a stoic sentinel amidst the rising questions surrounding them. Who was this new man? How did he fit into the web of Ry-Lan's machinations?

Each answer seemed to slip further away, obscured by the growing mystery. As the shadows deepened and the nearby roads hummed indifferently, Alex and Brian's minds intertwined with the same burning curiosity. They were one step closer to understanding, yet tantalizingly aware of the depths still left to explore.

* * *

The mental tug-of-war was intense—should they follow the stranger or stay and watch the enigmatic sphere? Finally, the pendulum swung towards action. Alex grasped the steering wheel, the decision crystallizing in an instant. "We should follow him," Alex declared, eyes steely with resolve.

With the decision made, Alex engaged the engine and eased the car forward, keeping just enough distance to remain inconspicuous. The shadowed figure moved with determined speed, his form growing smaller when the gap increased, but Alex was relentless.

They trailed him easily until he reached a path leading to a railway track. The environment shifted quickly from urban sprawl to the raw, industrial ambiance of the rail lines. Alex's pulse quickened; the railway was a dead end for the car.

"He's heading down the footpath. I can't follow him by car anymore," Alex informed Brian, glancing around. "You stay in the car. And I'll follow him on foot."

Alex pulled over to the side of the road, parked, and swiftly activated the location-sharing feature on WhatsApp, sending his live coordinates to Brian. "OK. My location's on. Let's stay in touch," Alex instructed before jumping out of the car.

"No worries," Brian assured, exiting the vehicle and moving around to the driver's side. "Stay safe."

Alex began the pursuit on foot, carefully maintaining a safe distance. The man was deceptively fast; his movements were those of an athlete. The chase led them along the railway track, with Alex avoiding the gravel path and running on the grass to remain quieter.

They moved into a housing estate, the transition marked by rows of tightly packed homes that breathed a different kind of life than the desolate tracks. Alex's breath began to come in shorter bursts, every sense heightened. The figure ahead seemed to slow, his head turning slightly as he scanned the array of parked cars.

Alex took cover behind a row of bushes, eyes narrowing as he watched the man searching for a suitable vehicle. The man's movements were calculated, every step taken with cautious precision. He finally settled on an older, less conspicuous model, hastening towards it with a practiced air.

Alex's heart pounded as he watched the stranger deftly break into the car, his movements smooth and economical. The engine purred to life moments later. The car edged forward slowly, gained speed, and then sped off, leaving only the faint smell of exhaust.

Alex took a deep breath from his hidden vantage point and thought through what he had seen. The stranger's actions were more than mere spectacle; they were breadcrumbs in a trail leading to deeper, darker truths. As the stolen car vanished into the night, Alex's mind whirred with possibilities and the resolve to uncover every shadowy detail laying ahead.

* * *

The stolen car disappeared around the corner, leaving a trail of uncertainty in its wake. Alex stood still for a moment, deliberating his next move. The man was gone, but the night held promises yet unfulfilled. Realizing the futility of continuing on foot, he pulled out his phone and quickly called Brian.

"Brian, he's gone. Stole a car and took off. What do I—"

Brian's voice cut through, firm and insistent. "Alex, it's nearing the critical window. You need to get back here. We can't miss Ry-Lan's appearance at 8:30. I'm already back at the car park."

Alex's gaze shot to the time displayed on the phone. Just fifteen minutes left. Panic fused with the thrum of adrenaline through his veins. "On my way," he replied, breathless.

Pocketing the phone, Alex sprinted back towards the railway tracks. Every step felt like it was dragging him through quicksand. The landscape blurred—a montage of steel rails, patches of overgrown grass, and dim streetlights casting eerie, long shadows. The rhythmic pulse of his footsteps became a metronome, marking each second as he inched closer to the car park—and to the unknown that awaited him there.

Bottle-brushed breaths punctuated Alex's ragged gasps, each intake as heavy as the questions spiralling in his mind. Had Ry-Lan already made his entrance? Would he be too late? He felt the pressure of these unknowns propelling him forward with a desperate urgency.

Bursting out onto the main road again, Alex barely made out the distant lights of the car park, its harsh concrete still as foreboding as ever. Time felt like an adversary, each second adding to the tension.

Alex's breath came in harsh, uneven gulps as he pushed himself harder. His legs burned with effort, muscles screaming in protest, but he couldn't afford to slow down. Every moment counted.

His phone buzzed, breaking his focus. A quick glance showed a message from Brian: "Hurry up. It's nearly 8:30 p.m."

Gritting his teeth, Alex increased his pace, the distance between him and the car park shrinking incrementally. He was tired but kept going, understanding the importance of getting back.

The edges of the car park loomed into view, bringing a fleeting sense of relief. Yet, the critical minutes ticked down relentlessly, and the true test lay just ahead. Alex knew that whatever awaited him held the key to unravelling the mysteries tethered to Ry-Lan, the strange sphere, and the man he had just witnessed.

His heart pounded with exertion and anticipation, knowing the clock was counting down fast. He was almost there, but would almost be enough?

Chapter 17

Alex's footsteps echoed through the desolate streets, his breaths coming in sharp, urgent bursts. Every part of his body screamed for rest, but his mind was a relentless taskmaster, driving him forward. Meanwhile, in the car park, Brian sat in the dimly lit interior of Alex's car, eyes glued to the enigmatic sphere. He clutched the phone tightly in his hand, its camera trained on the machine and the surrounding area, ready to capture whatever unfolded.

The digital clock on the car's dashboard ominously approached 8:30 p.m., each passing second adding to the tension. Brian's heart drummed a rapid beat, his knuckles white from gripping the phone.

Suddenly, the unsettling outline of the stranger's stolen car cut through the car park, headlights slicing through the darkness. Brian's pulse quickened. The man—the car thief Alex had chased through the housing estate, was back.

The car rolled to a smooth stop near the sphere, with its engine left running, a low hum filling the otherwise quiet car park. Brian's pulse quickened. The intruder exited the vehicle with an air of cold efficiency. He moved swiftly, eyes scanning for any signs of disturbance, but Brian remained unseen, cloaked in shadows and tense silence. Every nerve in Brian's body screamed for stillness, his breathing shallow as he recorded the scene.

The stranger headed to the sphere, the reflected light from the car's headlights giving his figure an almost ethereal glow. Without hesitation, he reached the machine and placed his hand on its surface. The machine responded with a low hum, the panel that had initially released the stranger sliding open to beckon him back inside.

Brian glanced at his phone. It was capturing it all—every shadow and flicker of light—as the intruder seamlessly re-entered the sphere. The display on his phone screen trembled slightly, his hands struggling to remain steady under the rising pressure of the anticipated climax.

The clock kept ticking, the digital numbers creeping ever closer to the critical moment of 8:30 p.m. Brian held his breath, unwilling to make even the slightest noise. His gaze darted between the car's clock and the machine, a perfect storm of expectation and dread brewing within him.

Was this part of Ry-Lan's planned appearance, or had they stumbled upon something far larger and more intricate than they had initially imagined? The questions gnawed at Brian, but there was no way to predict what would happen next.

As the final seconds trailed towards 8:30, the air grew heavier, charged with latent energy. Brian could feel the anticipation in every fibre of his being, an electric buzz crackling just beneath the surface of his skin. His instincts screamed that something significant would unfold at this precise moment.

Brian looked again at his phone. It was ready to capture whatever anomaly would follow. The final moment stretched into an eternity, defined by the rhythmic cadence of his heartbeat and the proximity of answers that remained just beyond reach.

All he could do now was wait, ensconced in the car, eyes wide with anticipation, hoping against hope that he was prepared for whatever revelation was about to unveil itself.

* * *

Contrary to their heightened expectations, the machine remained an inert monolith as the seconds blended into minutes. The digital clock on the car's dashboard ticked past the anticipated 8:30 p.m., adding to the frustrating silence. Brian's nerves were frayed, each passing second a taut wire ready to snap.

Time seemed to drag on as Brian's eyes darted between the clock and the motionless sphere. A soft click of metal and a faint hum finally broke the tension at 8:33 p.m. The sphere hatch slid open again, and out stepped Ry-Lan, his movements as deliberate and cautious as the previous man's.

Brian's breath caught in his throat. Ry-Lan's presence was a confirmation, a tangible bridge connecting the fragments of their fractured understanding. He watched intently, his phone recording every meticulous action with a steady lens.

Ry-Lan moved with a precision bordering on mechanical, scanning the surroundings with a surgeon's focus. He inspected the machine with a clinical interest, his hands trailing lightly over its smooth metallic surface. There was an air of command about him, an undeniable authority that seemed to hold the environment itself in check.

Brian crouched lower in the seat, trying to make himself as inconspicuous as possible while continuing to record. The atmosphere grew charged, every subtle movement of Ry-Lan laden with significance. He completed his assessment, stepped back, and turned his attention to the car left running by the first man.

In a fluid motion, Ry-Lan opened the car door and slid into the driver's seat. The stolen vehicle, already purring, registered his presence as it smoothly reversed and then accelerated out of the car park.

Brian's heart quickened with a fresh surge of adrenaline. His mind raced, calculating the risks and rewards. Determined not to lose this lead, he swiftly turned the car engine on, eyes fixed on Ry-Lan's retreating taillights. With deliberate caution, he began to follow, maintaining a discreet distance to avoid detection.

The pursuit was nerve-wracking. Brian's gaze flicked between Ry-Lan's car and the road ahead, every twist and turn a potential challenge. The quiet hum of his engine felt deafening in the otherwise still night, matching his rapid heartbeat.

"Come on, come on," Brian muttered under his breath, hands gripping the steering wheel with knuckles white as bone. Every decision, every split-second choice, weighed heavily on him. He couldn't afford to lose the trail now.

* * *

Brian fumbled as he picked up his phone to call Alex. The phone rang twice before Alex's breathless voice picked up on the other end.

"Brian, where are you? I can see him. He just passed me."

"I'm following him ... Wait, I can see you. I'll pick you up." Brian's voice was a tight wire of urgency. Every second counted in this unfolding drama.

Alex put his phone back in his pocket and waited at the roadside. Seconds later, his car pulled up beside him, with Brian driving. Alex threw open the door and jumped in, barely managing to close it before Brian accelerated again.

Rain began to patter lightly against the windshield, each drop creating a staccato rhythm that matched the tension in the car. The windshield wipers moved intermittently back and forth. With Alex now in the passenger seat, they renewed their pursuit, keeping a careful distance to avoid alerting Ry-Lan. The city of Darlington unfurled before them, its lights and sounds providing an interesting backdrop to their tense chase. After weaving through city streets, Ry-Lan's car finally slowed as they approached the town centre.

Brian and Alex exchanged a glance, understanding they were nearing the climax of their pursuit. Ry-Lan pulled into a town centre car park, its dim lighting casting long, ominous shadows. Brian quickly parked their car nearby, trying to avoid drawing attention.

Once out of the car, they followed Ry-Lan on foot, the rain now a drizzle, creating tiny rivers on the asphalt. He moved with the same fluid efficiency they had come to associate with him, leading them through the town centre towards a tawdry, cheap-looking nightclub.

Moving into the shadows, Brian started recording again, his phone's camera carefully watching Ry-Lan's every move. The nightclub's facade was gaudy under the streetlights, neon signs casting garish colours on the wet pavement. On the outside, a couple of bouncers eyed up the passersby.

Alex peered from his covert position, his breath misting in the cool air, eyes locked on Ry-Lan. He could see Ry-Lan standing in a shadow near the club's entrance, his presence a dissonant note in the otherwise mundane setting.

After about ten minutes, the club's double doors swung open, spilling three men onto the slick pavement. They moved with the casual swagger of those who believed the night was theirs to command. Alex's heart leapt into his throat as he recognised one of the figures.

"That's Ian Cooper," Alex whispered with excitement and dread. "The man I encountered earlier."

Brian's eyes narrowed, his grip on the phone tightening as he continued to record. A heavy stillness hung in the air as Ry-Lan, seeing the men approach, appeared to take something out of his pocket.

He put the object up to his face and wore it. It was a type of solid mask. The mask covered the lower half of his face and appeared to include earplugs that he inserted into each ear, holding the mask in place.

"What's happening?" Brian asked, mainly to himself.

"Stay low, stay quiet," Alex replied, his pulse racing. "We need to see what happens next."

The rain continued its gentle descent, a soft background murmur to the tension-laden scene unfolding before them. They remained hidden, eyes fixed on Ry-Lan as he prepared for a seemingly significant encounter.

* * *

Now masked and composed, Ry-Lan approached the group of men who had just exited the club. His movements were deliberate, exuding a controlled tension that mirrored the charged atmosphere.

Brian and Alex watched from their hidden vantage point, every muscle taut with anticipation. Brian's camera continued to record, capturing the moment Ry-Lan initiated the conversation. Even from a distance, the body language spoke volumes. The men were visibly uncomfortable, their postures defensive and rigid.

Alex tried but failed to catch anything of the conversation amidst the rain and distant city sounds. Ry-Lan appeared to be talking to the tallest of the group, but all three were responding. The men reacted with visible agitation, their faces contorting with displeasure. Ian Cooper, especially, seemed to grow more animated, his gestures wide and erratic.

"What do you think they're talking about?" Alex whispered, his eyes never leaving the scene.

"Whatever it is, they aren't happy about it," Brian replied softly, his focus unwavering.

The exchange lasted about five minutes. Ry-Lan's calm demeanour was in clear opposition to the growing agitation of the group. Suddenly, Ry-Lan stepped back, disengaging from the confrontation as quickly as it had begun. Without another word, he turned and began walking away, his figure merging with the shadows cast by the streetlights.

The men continued talking amongst themselves, their conversation now heated and fragmented. Alex and Brian could see the frustration simmering, threatening to boil over. Ian, at the centre of this storm, seemed to be the most decisive. Finally, with a determined set to his jaw, he broke away from the group and began to follow Ry-Lan at a distance.

Brian's camera captured it all, the lens now trained on Ian as he stalked after Ry-Lan. "He's following him," Brian murmured, excitement and concern colouring his voice.

"What do we do?" Alex asked, his mind teeming with the potential implications of this new development.

"Let's follow Ian," Brian replied firmly. "We know where they're ultimately going, and if we follow Ian, then we're basically following Ry-Lan anyway."

Keeping to the shadows, they trailed behind, carefully maintaining enough distance to remain unnoticed. The confrontation had set the stage for something far more significant, and as the rain continued to fall gently on the streets of Darlington, Alex and Brian knew they were on the cusp of uncovering deeper truths and even greater dangers.

* * *

The rain continued its gentle patter, adding an almost hypnotic rhythm to the tense atmosphere. Ian followed Ry-Lan with calculated steps, maintaining a cautious distance as Ry-Lan made his way back to the car he had arrived in. Ian got into a seemingly fortuitous nearby vehicle, clearly intent on continuing the pursuit.

Brian and Alex exchanged a quick glance, the unspoken agreement reaching an almost telepathic precision. "We should follow him," Brian said.

They moved swiftly back to their own vehicle, starting the engine with as little noise as possible. The windshield wipers worked in rhythmic unison with the rain, providing fleeting moments of clarity through the watery veil. They trailed Ian's car at a safe distance back towards the stadium.

Ian's car neared the stadium car park where they had initially spotted Ry-Lan. The tension in the air didn't dissipate; if anything, it grew denser with each passing second. Ian parked his car inconspicuously, his eyes fixed on Ry-Lan, who seemed completely unaware of his silent observer. In the muted glow of the streetlights, they watched as Ry-Lan re-entered the machine, the hatch absorbing him back into its metallic enclosure.

They observed from their distant vantage point, breaths shallow and synchronised with their rising tension. Ian seemed to come to a decision; his car slowly rolled forward, edging closer to the enigmatic sphere. The deliberate motion was laden with intent, but what that intent was remained a mystery.

Alex and Brian debated their next move, uncertainty and curiosity creating a fractured dialogue within the car's confines. "We should get closer," Brian suggested, eyes narrowing as he studied Ian's car.

"Too risky," Alex countered, shaking his head. "We can't afford to interfere, especially not now. We need to see this through from a safe distance."

They watched as Ian's car finally stopped a short distance from the machine. He remained inside, his silhouette barely discernible through the rain-streaked windows.

"What is he going to do?" Alex asked, his voice taut with anticipation.

Brian shook his head slightly. "We're about to find out."

Their car remained tucked in the shadows. They waited, eyes locked on the unfolding scene, senses tuned to even the subtlest of shifts. In that rain-drenched car park, the night promised answers—but also the spectre of new questions lurking just beyond the periphery of their understanding.

Chapter 18

The rain continued its unrelenting drizzle, each drop creating ripples that mirrored the uncertainties swirling in Alex and Brian's minds. Situated in the hidden confines of their car, they watched expectantly as Ian made his move.

Ian stepped out of his car, his cautious movements captured in the panorama of Brian's camera. He approached the sphere with an air of determination and trepidation. Alex and Brian could almost feel his scepticism and intrigue through the distance and the rain-streaked windows.

Ian trailed his fingers over the machine's surface, his touch almost reverential as he circled it. He paused occasionally, brow furrowing in what appeared to be frustration and fascination. Each meticulous inspection seemed to yield answers that only prompted more questions.

"What is he looking for?" Alex whispered, his breath fogging the car window slightly.

"Wish I knew," Brian replied, his eyes never leaving the scene. The camera lens focused intently on Ian, catching every subtle gesture, every shift in his posture.

Ian continued his circumnavigation of the sphere, his hands probing its seamless exterior for hidden secrets or perhaps a way in. His confusion grew increasingly evident; the subtleties of his body language painted a picture of a man wrestling with an enigma.

Finally, after one last lingering look, Ian sighed and turned back towards his car.

"Looks like he's given up," Alex said, astonishment tinging his voice.

"Or he's thinking things through," Brian countered, watching Ian closely as he climbed back into his vehicle. "This isn't over yet."

Ian sat in his car, hands gripping the steering wheel, his silhouette lit by the flicker of streetlights, his clearly frustrated demeanour an immediate change from the methodical patience he'd shown moments before. He seemed caught in an internal conflict, a churning sea of thoughts and plans, each struggling for dominance.

Brian lowered the camera slightly, the recording still ongoing. "Get ready. He might make another move."

The drama weighed heavily upon them. The machine, the repeated encounters, the almost theatrical tension—it all pointed to a larger scheme they had yet to fully grasp. They watched as Ian remained in his car, the rain relentlessly beating a rhythm on their windshield, providing a solemn backdrop to the unfolding drama.

As seconds transformed into long, stretched minutes, the two observers maintained their vigil. The rain, the machines, the people—they all seemed like pieces of an intricate, multi-dimensional puzzle, each click of the wipers marking another tick in the countdown to revelation.

* * *

Time stretched out, laden with anticipation and uncertainty. Suddenly, the stillness of the moment shattered.

Brian's eyes widened in shock. "Look, Alex, it's you."

Alex blinked, his breath catching in his throat as he turned his gaze towards the surreal scene unfolding before them. Emerging from the machine, there he was, arriving from two weeks ago.

"Woah! This is so surreal," Alex whispered.

They squinted through the rain-slicked haze, trying to make sense of what they were witnessing. The doppelganger moved with purposeful strides, and although it was difficult to see clearly, they could make out Ian's confused response from inside his car. His posture was rigid, and his movements jerky, clearly wrestling with the disbelief of what was unfolding before him.

Ian finally threw open his car door, his confusion evident even through the distorted view the rain provided. His posture stiffened, and then, with a sudden burst of motion, he approached the Alex doppelganger, his face a mask of shock and incredulity.

Alex watched with a surreal detachment as the confrontation unfolded exactly as he remembered it. His other self moved with an eerie precision, parrying Ian's attempts at engagement. Their heated exchange culminated in a brief struggle, a flurry of movement before Ian crumpled to the ground, unconscious, his body merging with the shadows cast by the dim streetlights.

"Did you really ..." Brian began, but Alex cut him off, the surreal nature of the tableau robbing him of coherence.

"Yes, you know I did. You've seen the video footage," Alex whispered, his voice strained with the pressure of it all.

Alex's twin paused for a moment, standing over Ian's unmoving body. Then, he retreated into the machine. The hatch closed smoothly behind him, the machine returning to its idle, enigmatic state as if nothing had transpired. And then it disappeared.

Ian lay still on the rain-slicked asphalt, the scene rendered almost ghostly by the persistent downpour.

"What just happened?" Alex asked, but this time, it was more a question for himself than for Brian. The sensation of déjà vu mixed with an out-of-body experience lingered, leaving him disoriented and uneasy.

Their breaths came quick and shallow as they kept vigil over the unconscious Ian. The rain continued its steady descent, each drop absorbing into the growing pool of their confusion and apprehension.

Alex's mind raced, the surreal experience of watching his past self interact with Ian merging with the immediate necessity of their next move. "We have a chance to get some answers," Alex said, breaking the heavy silence between them.

Brian's eyes remained locked on Ian's prone form. "We need to move fast. Whatever's happening here, we need to understand it."

They engaged in a rapid, hushed discussion, their voices barely rising above the rain's murmur. "You should go," Brian finally declared. "You've just interacted with him. You can try to continue from there."

Alex needed no convincing. He started the car and navigated closer to Ian's position. The headlights cut through the darkness, illuminating the scene with unsettling clarity. Ian remained on the ground, but the lights seemed to make him stir.

Alex quietly stopped the car just metres away. He stepped out, with his hooded jacket shielding him from the persistent rain. Taking a deep breath, he steeled himself for the encounter. It felt strange, not knowing how Ian would react to this continuation.

As Alex approached, Ian slowly came to, his disoriented gaze struggling to make sense of his surroundings. Alex knelt beside him, steadying his voice and projecting authority. "Ian, can you hear me? I'm Alex, a police officer. Are you OK?"

The mention of law enforcement seemed to snap Ian into a sharper focus, though confusion still clouded his features.

"A police officer?" Ian's voice was weak, tentative. "What ... what happened?"

"You tell me," Alex said, his tone firm but calm. "I found you unconscious. You need to tell me what happened and why you were here."

Ian's eyes flickered with the struggle to piece together his fragmented memories. He glanced towards where the machine had been and then back to Alex, suspicion and fear mingling in his expression. "I ... I saw someone. Wait, it was you! What's going on?"

"That's what we're trying to figure out," Alex replied, trying to keep his voice steady despite the surreal nature of the conversation. "Who did this to you? What happened?"

Ian rubbed his temples, trying to shake off the residual fog. "I don't understand. There was something here, and a man ... two men."

Alex's heart pounded. He was trying to stay relaxed and keep Ian calm, too. "Are you OK? Can you stand up?"

"My head hurts," Ian said, his voice gaining a bit of strength. "Ow, and my back." Ian got to his feet and rubbed his back and head.

"Where did you come from? And where did that ... thing go?" Ian asked, his voice shaky but gaining strength.

Maintaining his cover, Alex responded calmly, "I was here for the match earlier and then caught up with my buddy. We've been into town, and then I dropped him back at his car when we saw you."

Alex projected an air of authenticity and concern. "I want to help you, Ian. But first, I need you to help me understand what happened. Tell me about the man you were following and your conversation."

"How do you know my name?" Ian seemed even more perplexed.

"I looked at your driving licence in your wallet," Alex replied quickly. "That's what we do. So, what happened?"

Ian patted his pockets and felt for his wallet. Then he hesitated, glancing nervously at Brian, who remained in the car as a silent observer. Alex's steady gaze seemed to reassure him somewhat, and he reluctantly began speaking, "I was with two friends when a man approached us. He ... he had some kind of weird mask on. He was speaking in a foreign language and using it to translate his words. He seemed to know my mate, Steve, somehow."

Alex was listening carefully. "What did the man want with Steve?"

"He said Steve was sick. That he needed to go with him," Ian explained, his brow furrowing as he recalled the odd confrontation. "Steve had a few drinks, you know? He wasn't in the mood to listen. Thought this guy was just messing with him."

Alex encouraged Ian to continue. "And then?"

Ian swallowed, his voice dropping to a whisper. "Steve started to threaten the man. He wasn't having any of it. But the guy was insistent and said it was a matter of life and death. That's when things got heated."

Alex exchanged a quick glance with Brian, listening to every word. The pieces of the puzzle were starting to appear slowly, though much remained shrouded in mystery. What illness was Ry-Lan referring to? Why was it so urgent?

"Did this man say what was wrong with Steve?" Alex asked, his tone probing but cautious.

Ian shook his head, frustration and confusion evident in his expression. "No, he just kept insisting Steve had to go with him. That it was the only way to save him. Steve got angrier and more aggressive. And then ... the man turned round and left."

"Where did this happen? Here?" Alex knew the answer already but didn't want to give too much away.

"No, in town. I wasn't happy with all this. So, I followed the man back here. And he goes into some kind of machine, like a spaceship or summat. And now he's gone."

Alex stepped back, processing the information. The encounter was more than a mere confrontation. It hinted at a deeper, more complex situation—one that involved life-threatening stakes and a mysterious illness.

Alex finally spoke up, his voice calm and measured. "Ian, can you tell us where Steve is now?"

Ian looked at him, the fear and uncertainty raw in his eyes. "I—I don't know. After the argument, I left him there. He'll have gone to The Flyer, probably."

* * *

Alex stood there thinking about what Ian had said and what to do next. Ian stood beside him, shifting uncomfortably, still grappling with the jarring events of the night.

Ian broke the silence first, his voice subdued. "I wasn't drinking, you know. The guy was really weird, and it worried me. I decided to follow him to understand what he was really up to. But truth be told, I had no idea what I'd do if I caught up to him."

Alex was sympathetic, understanding the layers of fear and confusion Ian was grappling with. "I understand, Ian. You wanted to protect your friend and get to the bottom of whatever was happening. Anyone would do the same."

Ian looked at Alex, searching for some semblance of reassurance. "But now, it just seems even more confusing. What's really going on?"

Alex touched Ian's shoulder, trying to exude calm and confidence. "We're going to find out. But we'll need your help to piece this all together. Can we have your contact information and Steve's details, too, please? We need to follow up, officially."

Ian hesitated for a moment, showing his reticence. But the earnestness in Alex's voice swayed him. "Alright."

Ian recited his phone number and address, then looked up Steve's details. Alex jotted it all down, his head buzzing with the possibilities these new leads could open up.

As Ian relayed the last bit of information, Alex gave him a reassuring look. "Thank you, Ian. This will help us a lot. We'll check that Steve is okay and get to the bottom of this. Just try to stay safe and watch for anything unusual."

"I will. And ... thanks, I guess."

Without another word, Ian turned and walked back to his car, his figure framed by the dim glow of the streetlights. Alex and Brian watched as he got in, started the engine, and drove off into the night.

As the taillights of Ian's car disappeared into the distance, Alex turned to Brian, a new determination in his eyes. "There's no point trying to find Steve tonight if he's drunk and angsty. I can try to find him next week."

Brian agreed, clearly thinking through their next options. "Yes, of course. It's late now. Say, shall we meet up tomorrow to discuss our next options with the machine?"

"Sure. Would you like to come over to mine," Alex asked. "I'll cook us a nice English breakfast, and we can plan our next steps."

They climbed back into their own cars, the night's events leaving a heavy imprint on their thoughts. With Ian's contact information and the details of Steve's location, they had a new direction to pursue. The path ahead was uncertain, but the determination to uncover the truth had never been stronger.

Chapter 19

<u>Sun 21st April 2024</u>

Morning broke with a reluctant dawn, the grey sky mirroring the complexity of Alex's thoughts as he prepared for Brian's arrival. The previous night's events played on a loop in his mind, each replay fostering a deeper resolve to uncover the truths hidden behind Ry-Lan and the mysterious machine.

Brian arrived soon after 10 a.m., his expression reflecting the intensity with which he had approached the unfolding mystery. They settled in Alex's minimalist but comfortable living room, the air charged with the potential of new discoveries.

As they sipped their coffee, Alex broke the silence. "Brian, I've been thinking. What about the other entries in the machine's travel logs? They could be useful. Ones in the future will provide us another opportunity to watch Ry-Lan. And ones in the past could be useful too. We could see if the dates coincide with any major event."

"Yes, I was thinking the same thing. But I thought we were going to eat first," Brian said, mocking his friend.

"Alright, alright, I'll start cooking in a minute." Alex looked embarrassed. "What do you think about my idea, though?"

"Yes, it's a good one. As I said, I was thinking the same thing. I just wanted to wind you up. I'll go through my notes now and see what I can find," Brian said as he took out his notepad.

"What would you like? The works?" Alex asked as he headed to the kitchen.

"Yeah, great. I'm famished. I haven't eaten yet today."

Alex got to work at the stove, so pleased to be reacquainted with Brian again. It was just like old times back at university, and just like before, it was him in the kitchen.

* * *

Twenty minutes later, they were sitting at the kitchen table eating a hearty breakfast of bacon, sausages, scrambled eggs, and mushrooms, all on top of a couple of oatcakes.

"I found some interesting dates," Brian said through a mouthful of food. Some of them are quite special."

"Go on," Alex encouraged.

"November 22nd, 1963," Brian teased.

"I don't know why that's special. Should I?"

"It was the date of the assassination of John F Kennedy."

"Oh wow! I wonder why Ry-Lan would go there. To find out who did it? Or wait, do you think he was trying to stop it?"

"I doubt it. Because if so, then he wasn't successful." Brian had stopped eating now.

"How do you know?" Alex asked. "Oh, wait ... because if he'd have succeeded, then it would have changed history? What if he did it?"

"Again, that's not really likely. Is it?"

"No, I guess not. But wow, I wonder why he went there. Was it definitely Dallas that he went to?"

"I can't tell. But I'm pretty sure the date is correct. And here's another one—April 4, 1968. That's the date of the assassination of Martin Luther King Jr." Brian glanced at Alex. "There are some pretty significant dates in here. Here's another one: 30th April 1945. I checked. That's the date that Hitler committed suicide."

"Can I have a look at the list, please?" Alex asked and reached out his hand.

Brian handed the list of dates to Alex and got stuck back into his breakfast. Alex reviewed the list. Some dates felt familiar, though he wasn't sure why. Then he came across a date he had been hoping to find.

"Brian," Alex said, his voice conveying urgency and enthusiasm. "January 29, 2020!"

Brian looked at Alex, wondering why he'd chosen that one. "What happened on that date?"

"It's just before Covid. Mark was in the UK then."

Brian sensed what Alex was thinking. "You think it might be an opportunity to …"

"To go back, talk to him, maybe change things," Alex finished the sentence, the hope and pain mingling in his voice. "It's selfish, I know. But if we have this chance, we should take it, right?"

Brian was momentarily silent, considering. "I don't know. We've discussed this. It may not work out too well. You might make things worse."

"I can't see how they could be worse. I'm lost without him. It's killing me. In many ways, I'd rather it was me that was gone instead. And it's not fair on his wife and son either."

Brian placed a reassuring hand on Alex's shoulder. "Maybe you're right."

* * *

Brian started to consider the idea seriously. "There would be risks," he said after a while. "The virus was already spreading by then, but most people weren't aware of it."

A flicker of concern passed across Alex's face, but he quickly shook it off. "I've been vaccinated, and I've already had Covid a couple of times. So, I'm pretty immune already. No, I don't think that should stop us. Plus, I'd be there for a few hours at most."

Brian accepted Alex's answers, though the worry didn't completely leave his eyes. "Alright, but we need to be cautious. Prepare carefully. No unnecessary risks."

Alex squared his shoulders, his determination clear. "Agreed. Let's do this."

They gathered their gear and headed to Bingley farm, where the machine awaited them. The drive was quiet, each lost in their thoughts about what might happen. Upon arrival, the familiar sight of the farm brought a sense of purpose. The machine stood there, an unassuming sentinel holding the keys to their destiny.

Once inside the barrier, the atmosphere shifted to one of focused preparation. Alex rummaged through his backpack, ensuring he had everything for a brief but significant journey to 2020. He'd had the foresight to bring a warm coat as he'd recalled January's biting chill that year. For a moment, the thought of re-experiencing those wintery days brought a nostalgic smile to his face.

Brian was nearby, checking the machine and then selecting the destination from the history logs. "Everything looks good here," he announced. "Remember, Alex, you will arrive when Ry-Lan leaves. So, check your cameras again before you get out. And come back as quickly as you can."

Alex put on his coat, aware of how significant his next move was for himself and history. "Understood. I'll be quick."

Brian turned his attention to Alex and checked his bodycam as he spoke to him. "Any problems, just come straight back. OK?"

Alex placed a reassuring hand on Brian's shoulder. "I will. Thanks, mate. Hopefully, before you know it, I'll be back with some answers."

With a wave goodbye, Alex closed the hatch and activated the machine. Its humming grew louder, and then Alex felt that familiar sensation as the machine jumped back in time.

Wed 29th January 2020

Alex checked the external cameras. From what he could see, he was in a remote, wooded area. It looked cold outside, and there were no signs of life. He exited the machine and checked the outside just as he'd seen Ry-Lan do.

The immediate chill of the winter air hit him, and he drew his coat tighter around his body as he surveyed his surroundings. Tall trees, bare branches outlined against the wintry sky, surrounded a tranquil lake with an almost surreal stillness.

Shivering slightly, Alex took his first tentative steps, the crunch of frozen leaves underfoot the only sound breaking the silence of the woods. The canopy of naked branches above cast eerie shadows as he navigated through the underbrush, each step marked by the occasional slip on patches of ice hidden beneath layers of fallen foliage. He walked for what seemed an eternity, the dense forest revealing few signs of civilization. His breath came in visible, misty clouds, with each exhale a reminder of the cold, the isolation, and the uncertainty of his predicament.

The forest seemed to stretch endlessly, every hill and hollow blending into a monotonous repetition. Alex's disappointment grew with each passing minute, the realisation that he had landed far from his intended destination gnawing at his resolve. This was meant to be a moment of closure, a chance to change his past and perhaps his future. Instead, he was lost in an unfamiliar, frigid wilderness.

Finally, after what felt like an age, the trees became less dense. He noticed a faint rumbling, growing steadily louder as he forged ahead. Pushing through the last stretch of underbrush, he stumbled onto the edge of a busy motorway. The difference between the chaotic rush of vehicles and the hushed quiet of the woods was jarring.

Alex scanned the area, taking in the sight of cars and lorries speeding by. A profound disappointment settled over him; this was not the UK. His pulse quickened as he tried to orient himself, the reality of his unexpected location sinking in. He walked along the motorway's edge until he found a sign: Valmadrera.

Confused and increasingly concerned, Alex pulled out his phone and opened his map application. The letters and lines on the screen unmistakably placed him in Italy, far from where he'd hoped to be.

The enormity of this realisation hit him like a cold wave. He had no passport or money and was in a foreign country. Alex started to think through the practicalities of reaching Mark in person. He would need to catch a plane, traverse international borders, and navigate the red tape—all without essential travel documents—it seemed complicated and nearly impossible.

He considered heading back to get better prepared. Yet, the portal to return wasn't readily available, nor was retreating within his nature. Frustrated and with the winter wind whipping through his coat, Alex leaned back against the nearest tree to gather his thoughts.

He decided to continue. If fate had led him to this specific point in Italy, there had to be a reason. Resolving to use his accidental detour, he began walking along the motorway's edge, heading towards Valmadrera. The road stretched before him, and each step carried the chill of uncertainty and a renewed determination to find meaning and purpose in this unexpected journey.

With each step, he wrestled with the disappointment, transforming it into resolve. The silent guardians of trees flanked his path, bearing witness to his stumble through time and place. Alex pressed forward, determined to uncover whatever clues his detour might hold, one step closer to rewriting his story. His journey, though diverted, was far from over.

* * *

As he pressed on, the sight of a small village slowly emerged from the fog. Ancient stone buildings, seemingly huddled together for warmth, lined narrow cobblestone streets. The juxtaposition of modern cars parked outside historic façades created an unintentional blend of past and present. His eyes were drawn to a modest shop, its quaint wooden sign swaying slightly in the breeze: "Emporio di Rossi."

Drawing his coat tighter around himself, Alex pushed open the shop's heavy door, a bell tinkling above his head announcing his arrival. Inside, the comforting warmth enveloped him, carrying the aromas of cured meats, fresh bread, and espresso. A stocky, middle-aged man stood behind the counter, arranging various cheeses. He looked up, his eyes narrowing slightly as he took in Alex's dishevelled appearance.

"Buongiorno," the man greeted with a trace of suspicion.

"Good morning," Alex replied, relief flooding his voice. "Do you speak English?"

"Si. A lee-ttle. 'ow can I help you?" the shopkeeper responded, his accent thick but his tone soft.

Alex spoke slowly for the shopkeeper. "Where is the nearest police station?"

The shopkeeper, Rossi, scratched his head thoughtfully. "There is-a police station, but I think I can help-a you better." He pulled out his mobile phone and made a call. "My friend-a Marco is police. He speaks-a good English. He will know what to do."

Within minutes, Rossi was speaking rapidly into the phone, occasionally casting sympathetic glances at Alex. After a brief conversation, he handed the phone to Alex, mouthing, "Marco."

"Hello, this is Alex," he said, trying to hide the desperation in his voice.

"Hello, Alex. I'm Officer Marco Bianchi. Please tell me what you need," came the officer's measured, reassuring voice.

Alex explained his urgent need to contact his brother and the unusual circumstances of his travel. There was a moment of silence on the other end of the line before Marco responded with calm authority. "I understand. Make your way to the police station in Lecco. I will meet you there and help you make the call."

Marco then gave Alex the directions from the shop to the police station.

Rossi offered Alex some bread and cheese for the journey. "You look-a like-a you need it," he said with a kind smile. His unexpected kindness touched Alex, adding a flicker of hope to an otherwise bleak day.

"Thank you," Alex replied gratefully. He set off again, buoyed by the prospect of speaking to his brother.

The journey to Lecco was uneventful but exhausting. The winding roads, lined with leafless trees, eventually led him to a quaint town nestled on the shores of Lake Como. He followed Marco's directions to the small, unassuming police station, its exterior plain against the backdrop of the picturesque town.

Marco was waiting in the reception area, his uniform impressive but different from the kind that Alex was used to. He approached Alex with a hand extended in greeting. "You must be Alex. Come through, let's get you sorted."

The police station was warm and functional, buzzing softly with the day's duties. Marco led Alex to a back room and offered him a seat. "Now, about your brother," Marco said, leaning forward, his expression earnest.

Alex relayed his brother's phone number and the urgency of his mission. Understanding Alex's plight, Marco picked up the phone without hesitation. Despite the lingering uncertainty and surreal nature of his journey, Alex felt a glimmer of hope.

The call went through. As the phone rang, Alex's heart pounded with the desperation and hope of a man travelling through time and space for this moment. The anticipation was almost unbearable, and he clung to the absurd sliver of faith that perhaps, just perhaps, the universe was aligning in his favour.

* * *

The phone held in Alex's trembling hand felt unnaturally heavy, the receiver pressed against his ear, a lifeline to a voice he had only heard in his dreams and memories for so long. The moments stretched out interminably as he waited for an answer to his call. Each second felt like an hour, and the potential consequences of what he was about to divulge threatened to overwhelm him. He squeezed his eyes shut, willing himself to focus, to steady his racing heart and frantic thoughts.

What do I tell him first? Alex pondered. His mind raced through possible openings. He pictured Mark's familiar face, sceptical and analytical, and mentally prepared for the inevitable disbelief. "Mark, it's me, Alex. You're going to think I'm insane, but I'm calling from the future." The words played in his head, sounding ludicrous even to him.

No, no. Too abrupt. He'll think I'm joking or, worse, delusional. I need to ease him into it. He took a deep breath and thought again, picturing a calmer, more measured approach. "Mark, please hear me out. I know this sounds impossible, but I'm speaking to you from 2024. Something incredible has happened. Let me explain."

Alex glanced at the faded posters on the police station walls, their warnings and public service announcements appeared to be reminders of the mundane world from which he was now separate.

The quiet hum of the police station and the distant murmur of voices all blended into a single, muted backdrop. He shifted uncomfortably, feeling the weight of his coat, the smell of worn wood and aged paper in the room merging with the metallic tang of old radiators. But that alone won't convince him, Alex thought. He needs to understand why I've contacted him now, specifically.

His heart pounded, each beat a countdown to when Mark would finally answer. How do I make him believe that this isn't a prank? He rehearsed Mark's sceptical questions in his mind, preparing responses that could validate his outlandish claims. "Check the news. Look up any early reports about mysterious visitors or unexplained phenomena. These should ease your doubts."

"Hello, Mark speaking?" came his brother's familiar voice.

Everything Alex had mentally rehearsed came into sharp focus. The next few moments would determine not just the trajectory of his mission but perhaps the fate of those he loved most. Steeling himself, he prepared to speak quickly and convincingly, a lifeline of hope stretched across time.

"Hey Mark, it's Alex. It's good to hear your voice again." Alex indicated to Marco with a thumbs-up gesture that he was through to his brother, and then, putting his hand over the receiver, he asked Marco if it was OK to have a little privacy.

"Si," Marco said and left the room, leaving Alex to speak with his brother alone.

Chapter 20

"So, Mark. How have you been?" Alex asked, trying to keep his tone light despite the urgency brewing inside him.

"I'm doing alright. I'm back home for a while now. I'm not sure how long for. What about you? What's going on?" Mark's voice carried the warmth and casualness of sibling familiarity. Alex was tense and anxious, trying not to reveal his tightly wound nerves.

A brief silence settled as Alex gathered his thoughts. "Actually, a lot has happened. It's been quite the adventure recently."

"That sounds intriguing," Mark said with a chuckle. "So, where are you calling from? Are you calling from abroad?"

"Believe it or not, I'm in Italy," Alex admitted, bracing for the immediate flood of questions that would follow.

"Italy?" Mark repeated, incredulity colouring his voice. "What the hell are you doing in Italy? And how did you get the time off work for that?"

"Mark, it's complicated. I need you to listen carefully. What I have to say is incredible, and you're going to find it hard to believe. But I need you to trust me," Alex said, his voice edging into seriousness.

"Alright, hold on a second. Let me go somewhere quieter," Mark replied. The muffled sounds of movement and distant chatter ceased. "Okay, I'm settled now. What's going on?"

Alex took a deep breath, the words heavy on his tongue. "Mark, I know this will sound impossible, but I've travelled back from the future. Specifically, from the year 2024. I'm the Alex you know—your brother—but I've come from 2024."

Mark's incredulity was replaced by a tense silence. "What are you talking about? Are you okay? Have you lost your mind?"

"I haven't, Mark. I know it sounds insane but I'm deadly serious. I need you to take what I'm saying at face value and allow me to explain," Alex implored, the insistence in his voice becoming more pronounced.

"Tell me why you're in Italy then. How did you end up there?" Mark's voice suggested scepticism and genuine concern.

"I landed here by mistake. I didn't mean to come to Italy; it was a miscalculation. But that's beside the point right now. I need to tell you something important," Alex explained, slowly.

Mark sighed, frustration mingling with confusion. "I don't understand. You're not making any sense."

"Yes, I know it's difficult to believe. Let me take it slow. I am your brother Alex. I have travelled back in time from the year 2024, and I need to tell you about something that will happen in your future so that you can avoid it," Alex conveyed, each word heavy with conviction.

The line fell silent again as Mark processed the information. "Alex, this is too much. Can you prove it? Can't you just come round so that we can talk this through properly?"

"I can't, Mark. As I said, I'm in Italy," Alex repeated, feeling the frustration of repeating his improbable predicament.

"Right, Italy. Why does this get weirder by the minute?" Mark muttered, half to himself. "This isn't some kind of prank, is it?"

"OK, look. I'm going to tell you some things from your future so that you can believe me when they come true. Is that fair?" Alex began.

"Go on," Mark replied, his scepticism obvious yet reflecting curiosity.

"Today is 29th January 2020, right? So, currently, a virus is sweeping through the world. The virus is going to be called COVID-19. Soon, governments around the world, including the UK, will declare a national emergency. Then, the UK will go into lockdown. People won't be allowed out of their houses," Alex explained, trying to keep his voice calm and factual.

Mark's silence on the line suggested he was processing this information. Finally, he said, "Okay, I've heard a bit about a virus from China on the news. Is that it? It's just a fuss about nothing, though. Isn't it?"

"Mark, that's it. That's COVID-19. It's not just another sensationalist news story. It's going to escalate incredibly quickly. Soon, hospitals will be overwhelmed, schools will close, and entire cities will be under strict quarantine," Alex pressed on, hoping his brother could sense the urgency in his words.

"I don't know. You really expect me to believe all of this? How can I be sure?" Mark retorted, still sounding unsure.

"OK. You want more?" Alex continued. "The British Prime Minister, Boris Johnson, will contract the virus soon after. He'll be admitted into intensive care and nearly die, but then he recovers. Later, the same happens to the US President, Donald Trump. This is real, Mark. This is what's going to happen."

Mark's incredulity seemed to wane slightly. "And this is all going to happen soon? This year? And you're telling me this so that I can avoid it?"

"Yes. No. Wait. That's not the point. I mean, yes, the virus is deadly. Lots of lives will be lost. Hundreds of thousands. Millions, even. But you're fine," Alex was a little flustered. "I mean, no, you do catch it. But you're fine. Lots of people catch it, and they're fine. It mainly affects the elderly."

"But that's not why I've called," Alex tried to get the conversation back on track.

"What do you mean?" Mark asked, confusion and a hint of apprehension in his voice.

"It's what happens after that which truly concerns me. In 2022, you're scheduled for a military tour in Iraq. It's imperative you don't go."

"Alex, you know I can't just leave the army. It's my duty and my life's work. Besides, what are you suggesting—desertion?" Mark's voice wavered between disbelief and defensiveness.

"Listen to me, Mark. I'm not asking you to abandon your commission. I know how much duty means to you. But your life is at stake. I've seen what happens. If you go on that tour, you'll disappear in a bad way," Alex's voice was thick with emotion. "You need to find a way to get out of it."

Alex gulped before he continued. "I'm sorry to say this, but you need to disappear on your own, to go into hiding. No one must know where you are."

Mark was silent momentarily, grappling with the enormity of what his brother was asking. "I can't believe what you're saying. You're telling me to abandon my career and go into hiding? You want me to cut off all contact with our family and friends?"

Mark became really angry. "Who are you? Do you even know me at all?"

"Mark," Alex said firmly, but his voice was gentle. "I understand the scale of what I'm asking. But I love you. I'm trying to save your life. You need to believe me. If you go on that tour, then you won't come home. I'm from the future, Mark. I've seen what happens. You need to trust me."

Mark's breath hitched, the reality of Alex's plea gnawing at his resolve. "But Alex, how could I do that to Kate? To Ethan? Just to vanish?"

"I can't begin to imagine how hard this must be for you, Mark. But think about it this way: if you don't listen, you won't be able to serve our country or see your family anyway. I've seen the future—I'm trying desperately to save your life. It is a major sacrifice, I know. But if you listen to me, then you will see them again. If you don't, then ..." Alex couldn't finish the sentence.

Mark let out a frustrated sigh. "Damn it, Alex. You're putting me in an impossible position. This is crazy. There must be another way."

"There isn't. You need to trust me. It's dangerous enough me coming back in time to tell you. We cannot risk any greater consequences. You need to disappear and not reappear until after the time in the future that I'm from," Alex insisted, his words desperate yet resolute. "Then things will work out."

"When are you from? When would I need to hide until?"

"April 2024. I'm from April 2024. Actually, let's just say May 2024. You can come out of hiding after the 1st of May 2024. Then it will be safe again."

Mark's interest seemed to shift suddenly. "OK, Alex, I'll consider what you're asking, but I need more proof first. Tell me then, if you're really from the future, about Leeds United. Are we gonna get back to the Premier League this year?"

Alex smiled to himself, knowing how to leverage their shared passion for football. "Alright, Mark. I've got this. Yes. Leeds do get promoted this year, as champions. It's a phenomenal season for us

Leeds fans. Well, apart from the virus, of course. Pretty soon you won't be able to go to any of the games. But yes, we get promoted."

Mark seemed interested. "Then what? Do we win the Prem?"

"Calm down, bruv. Let's be realistic. Next year, they will have a good season. They finish in the top half, but then, it kind of falls apart. The year after, they narrowly avoid relegation on the last day of the next season and, then, unfortunately, get relegated the year after. They're back in the Championship now, where I'm from," Alex explained, feeling the familiar pang of disappointment that came with recounting this.

Mark absorbed this information, his tone now measured and thoughtful. "That's ... very interesting. What about the Euros, then? How do England do?"

Alex hesitated for a moment to think. "Erm, if I remember right, the Euros got delayed because of the virus."

"Oh, yeah, the virus," Mark sounded a little sarcastic. "Of course."

Alex ignored him. "Yeah, they were delayed by a year, but when they finally happened in 2021, England made it to the final. They faced Italy, and it was decided on penalties. But we lost."

"Typical," Mark sighed, a mixture of frustration and pride in his voice.

Alex's voice brightened slightly. "Oh, but then, the women's team won their Euros. It was actually pretty cool. Beat Germany in the final. 2-1 it was. The lasses scored the winner in injury time."

Mark seemed to be enjoying the conversation now. "Nice one. OK, now tell me about the American election. Does Trump win again this year?"

"No, Joe Biden wins. Wow. That was a mental time. Trump, eh. He's quite a character," Alex replied, chuckling to himself.

Mark exhaled slowly, absorbing the plethora of predictions. "Alright, Alex. I'll tell you what. If these things come true, then I'll do what you ask."

"Thank you, Mark. I know it sounds crazy. But please remember, I'm telling you all this for a reason. You must not tell anyone, though. No one. Not even Kate. When they ask you to go to Iraq in 2022, just say your goodbyes like normal and travel. But somehow, you then need to escape and go into hiding. And then stay off the grid until May 2024. You've got that?" Alex reiterated, hoping his brother couldn't just hear his words but feel their urgency.

Mark's voice wavered with concern and curiosity. "But how am I supposed to reappear again after that date? What do I tell everyone? How can I get away with it?"

Alex took a deep breath, steadying himself. "Just tell everyone you were held hostage and managed to escape. Trust me on this. I'm from then. It will sound plausible enough. People will be relieved you're alive. I know what I'm asking is a really big deal, but you can do it. And once it's over, you can reclaim your life, even though it means missing a couple of years. You'll still be alive and can rejoin your family again."

"Okay, okay," Mark sighed. "I'll do it. I'll figure out how to go off-grid like you said. I just hope you're right. This had better be worth it, Alex."

"It will be. Trust me. As soon as you start seeing these things come true, you'll know. Just promise me you'll follow my instructions," Alex responded softly. "And definitely do not speak to me about it back in 2020, I mean, now. Don't speak to the me who is back in the UK. I must not know about this. You understand?"

"Yes, I understand. Take care of yourself, Alex," Mark said with newfound determination.

As the call ended, Alex sat back, feeling relief and apprehension. He had done all he could to alter his brother's fate, planting the seeds of action and trust. Now, only time would tell if those seeds would blossom into the changes needed to steer Mark away from danger and reshape their future.

For the first time since embarking on this convoluted journey, Alex felt a glimmer of hope. The responsibility hadn't lessened, but knowing Mark was willing to take such drastic steps provided a much-needed anchor against the swirling uncertainty. With his heart beating a steady rhythm of resolve, Alex prepared to face whatever came next, bolstered by the promise that perhaps, just perhaps, they were rewriting their shared destiny for the better.

Chapter 21

Alex stood up, every muscle in his body weary but slightly lighter. He walked out into the main area of the police station, where Officer Marco Bianchi awaited him, a questioning look on his face.

"Everything sorted?" Marco asked, genuine concern lacing his words.

Alex smiled in response. "Yes, thank you, officer. Your help has been invaluable."

Marco gestured towards the door. "Can I give you a ride somewhere?"

The offer was tempting, but Alex shook his head. "I appreciate it, but I'm fine."

Marco's eyes widened slightly, but he didn't press the issue. "Alright then. Take care of yourself, signore. And good luck."

Alex extended his hand, and they shared a firm handshake. "Thank you. For everything."

The crisp air outside bit Alex's cheeks as he began his solitary trek back to the time machine. The late afternoon light cast long shadows, the chill of the winter day a constant presence. The conversation had really washed him out, and he felt really tired now. Perhaps he should have taken the lift after all. Eventually, he found his way back to where he had joined the road earlier.

After what seemed ages, Alex finally navigated the woods and found the hidden spot where the machine awaited him, still and silent as always. He made a mental note to pin the location on a future map to make it easier to find again.

Stepping back into the machine's familiar confines, Alex relished the controlled, temperate environment. The hum of dormant systems greeted him like an old friend, offering a refuge from the chaotic unpredictability of the outside world.

With practised motions, Alex activated the return sequence. As before, the machine's hum grew into a resounding throb of potential energy. As he initiated the final steps, he reflected on the significance of his journey. His brother's safety and possible ripple effects on the future—all hinged on the success of his actions today.

The machine began to vibrate gently, the lights flickering before stabilising into a steady glow. Alex's heart matched the rhythmic pulses, the sensation familiar and exhilarating. Closing his eyes, he took a deep breath, readying himself for the jump.

With a final thrum, the time machine completed the jump. Alex opened his eyes as the noise subsided.

Stepping out of the machine, Alex was greeted by the familiar sights and sounds of his own time. The air was warmer again, and the beauty of an English countryside soothed him. His heart tightened as he thought of Mark, now equipped with the knowledge and warnings that might just save his life.

<u>Sun 21st April 2024</u>

Brian was waiting for Alex as expected, his eyes lighting up with curiosity and concern the moment Alex came out.

"Alex! You made it back. How did it go?" Brian's voice was eager, unable to mask the undercurrent of worry likely building during Alex's brief absence.

"It was intense, Brian. I was transported to Italy of all places. I didn't know what to do. I thought about coming back, but in the end, I decided to press on. I found a police station and managed to place a phone call to Mark," Alex paused, out of breath.

"Go on," Brian encouraged.

"I told Mark that I was from the future."

"Did he believe you?"

"I think so. Well, not at first. But I think I managed to convince him. And I told him to avoid his deployment to Iraq in 2022."

Brian was hanging on his every word. "And? How did he take it?"

"OK, I think," Alex replied, a faint smile playing on his lips as he remembered the conversation. "He was sceptical at first, but I think I convinced him. He said he would try to avoid the deployment. But convincing him to go into hiding until now was a tougher sell. In the end, though, he said he'd do it."

Brian exhaled, visibly relieved. "That's good. It's a lot for him to digest, but it sounds like you handled it well."

"Thanks," Alex said, though his voice held unresolved tension. "I just hope it's enough. There's still so much at stake."

"Well, I guess we'll find out soon," Brian noted. "If it worked, he'll appear again soon, right?"

"Yes, I guess you're right." Alex became emotional as he considered the possibility.

A brief silence hit them after what had happened. Had they really changed the past? They would find out soon enough.

"You're shivering," Brian said. "Let's get you in the car to warm up."

Soon, they were sitting in Alex's car with the engine running. Alex was the first to speak, "With all that's been going on, and now my problems with Mark, I haven't thought to ask you about your troubles. Have you and Emily spoken to Danny?"

Brian clutched his forehead and expelled a heavy breath. "Time has been a little hard to find, what with work, Ry-Lan, and the machine, and I can sense Emily getting uptight about it. Look, I'm going to need to be there when Danny gets home from school today."

Alex nodded emphatically, feeling a stab of guilt that his desire to see his brother safe was cutting into his friend's family time. "I understand … I'm sorry I …"

"Not at all," Brian broke in. "Remember, we're in this together. It's just that I need to devote some family time to later today."

"Fine," Alex said, seeing Brian's dilemma and grateful for his support, "so what's next? We still have the mystery with Ry-Lan to solve."

Brian smiled at the mention of Ry-Lan. "Yes, that's exactly where we need to refocus our efforts. I'm still not sure what to do. We still have no idea why he's here or how to help him."

Alex thought for a moment. "We've seen that his movements coincide with some significant historical dates. Perhaps there's a pattern or a purpose we're missing."

* * *

Brian, ever the thoughtful and analytical partner, stretched in his seat, expression contemplative. "Alex, I've been thinking. If we use the machine's logs to ascertain Ry-Lan's next appearances, we can keep learning more about him and his mission."

Alex's eyes lit up at the prospect. The chance to engage more directly with the mysteries surrounding Ry-Lan was exactly the pivot of focus he needed. "That's a brilliant idea, Brian."

Brian paused, deep in thought. "The logs have always displayed a pattern. They don't just jump to any point in history—they seem attracted to significant events. Obviously, where he's coming from, he already knows the significant events from what is our future."

Alex understood. "You're right. You know, I think we're done here for the day. Let's head back to mine, and we'll get the kettle on while we discuss what to do next."

Brian smiled. "Sounds like a plan. A hot drink would be perfect right now."

"So, tell me more about your time in Italy," Brian said as they pulled onto the narrow country road. "How did you manage to get hold of Mark?"

Alex chuckled, shaking his head at the sheer improbability of it all. "It was quite the experience, let me tell you. I landed in the middle of nowhere and had to navigate through a forest to find civilization. I then followed a road until I came to a shop. The owner didn't speak much English but knew someone who did. A policeman, in fact. He gave me directions to the police station and helped me place a call to Mark."

Brian whistled softly. "That's something. Sounds like a movie plot. How did Mark take it all? The time travel, the warning?"

"He was sceptical, of course. But I was able to tell him enough information about his future to convince him, I think," Alex explained, focusing on the winding road ahead.

Brian nodded as they drove over a small bridge. "You did well, Alex. Really well. It must have been challenging holding it together with everything on the line."

"It was," Alex admitted, his voice revealing the stress of recent events. "But knowing that I tried at least gives me some peace of mind. And it was so fantastic to speak to him and hear his voice. It's all down to him now. Meanwhile, we can focus on Ry-Lan and determine our next move."

The drive back to Alex's home was peaceful, and the rolling countryside provided reliable comfort. As they reached Alex's home, the familiar sight brought a sense of relief. They stepped inside, and Alex quickly put the kettle on.

* * *

They settled at the kitchen table, each with a steaming cup in hand, and the aroma of freshly brewed tea filled the room.

Brian pored over the machine's logs on his laptop, lost in concentration. The soft click of the keyboard keys filled the room as he sorted the locations in date order, making the entries easier to read. Alex was beside him, watching patiently.

"OK, here is the stadium location that you jumped to," Brian said, pointing to an entry on the screen. "And this is the next one chronologically. It's October this year. We know when, but not where, of course."

Alex counted on his fingers as he examined the entry. "That's six months away. And look at the one after that—it's not until 15 months later. Then let's get ready. I can travel to the October destination and find its location."

Brian had a hint of concern in his expression. "Alex, you know it could be anywhere. Anywhere in the world."

"Of course," Alex said, his voice steady. "And I'm ready for it. Let's get the gear together and do the jump today."

Brian sighed. "C'mon mate, we've had enough stress for one day, and I need to be going. Let's plan it carefully. We shouldn't rush this."

Alex frowned but saw the logic in Brian's words. "OK, but soon, though. I want to do this as soon as possible. We don't know how long we'll have the machine before someone else discovers it."

"How about next Saturday? That will give us time to plan properly. I can meet you at the farm at 9 a.m."

Alex knew this was a good idea. "Next Saturday it is. We'll meet at the farm and do it."

They spent a few more minutes discussing the finer details of their plan, ensuring they had thought of everything necessary for a successful reconnaissance mission. Then Brian headed home, his thoughts now occupied with his and Emily's coming talk with their son.

The week passed quickly for Alex, who had to attend a work training course that took up most of his time. The busy schedule helped keep his mind occupied, and Saturday had arrived before he knew it.

Sat 27th April 2024

The morning sun broke through the clouds, casting a golden hue over the rolling hills as Alex made his way to the farm that still housed the machine. The fresh scent of dew-laden grass filled the air, a reminder that he was at home here in the countryside. Arriving just before 9 a.m., he parked his car and took a moment to take in the familiar surroundings.

Alex was dressed warmly, wearing a thick coat to anticipate the unknown conditions he might face. His backpack contained a hat, gloves, and water. He approached the machine, feeling the usual excitement building.

By 9:20 a.m., Brian arrived. "Sorry I'm late," he said. "They closed the A1 this morning. We had a massive detour."

"No worries," Alex replied, ready to get started but mindful of Brian's troubles at home. "I was just enjoying the views. "How are things at home – the problem with …"

Brian shook his head with a smile. "The problem turned up on our doorstep before we'd a chance to talk matters through with him. New girl in class – happens they'd fallen out, but she came to apologise. So all lovey-dovey again." He paused, giving Alex a wry look, "Until the next time. Part of growing up, I suppose." Quickly dismissing the matter, he said, "Now let's push on and get you checked over."

Brian paused to compose himself before examining Alex, ensuring the bodycam was working. "Everything looks good," he said with satisfaction.

Brian used the card to enter the machine and programmed it to the correct destination. "Alright, it's all set," he confirmed, stepping aside to let Alex enter.

Brian handed the card to Alex. "Don't forget this. You'll need it to lock the machine when you're there."

Alex climbed into the machine, strapping himself in securely. He closed the hatch, aware of the importance of the mission. The accustomed hum of the machine surrounded him as he begun the transfer.

The machine whirred to life, lights flickering as the energy built up for the jump. Alex felt the sensation of being lifted out of time and space, the air around him vibrating with potential.

As the world around him blurred and then sharpened into focus, Alex knew he was about to dive into another uncertain adventure into their unfolding mystery. The answers they sought were out there, waiting to be discovered, and he was ready to face whatever came next.

Chapter 22

<u>Tue 15th October 2024</u>

The machine's hum faded, signalling its arrival at the new destination. Strapped securely in his seat, Alex took a deep breath before unfastening the harness. He turned on the machine's external cameras to get a look around.

Everything seemed quiet. There was some kind of obstruction at the rear and barren terrain to the front. It seemed safe to exit. Alex climbed out of the machine and stepped down to a ledge below.

The machine was in a secluded location, nestled within a natural alcove formed by towering rock formations. The cleft between the rocks provided excellent camouflage, concealing the machine from any casual observer. Three walls of the machine were pressed against the rough, craggy surface of the mountain while the door opened to a downward-sloping terrain.

It was bright outside, and it took his eyes a while to adjust to the bright sunlight. When they had adjusted, he took his small notepad out of his pocket and wrote 'sunglasses'. Next time he would be even better prepared.

The warm air enveloped him, prompting him to leave his thick coat behind inside the machine. The terrain before him sloped gently downward, leading into a vista of warm, earthy hues and sparse vegetation.

Absorbing the surroundings, Alex noted the unusual geological features. The rocky alcove provided a perfect hiding spot for the machine, ensuring it remained unnoticed. He could hear the distant call of birds and the rustle of dry grass in the gentle breeze.

He carefully navigated the uneven terrain, keeping a vigilant eye on his surroundings. The rugged beauty of the scenery captivated him, but he remained focused on the mission. As he moved further down the slope, the terrain revealed more of its character. Sparse vegetation gave way to clusters of scrubby bushes and patches of dry grass. The landscape stretched out below, a vast expanse of rocky terrain dotted with occasional patches of yellow. The dry air carried a faint scent of earth and sun-baked stone.

Alex paused momentarily, removing his water bottle from his bag and taking a sip of water. He looked around, trying to get his bearings. He had no immediate landmarks to identify his location, but the rugged terrain and the intense sunlight hinted at a mountainous desert or arid region.

Determined to gather more clues, Alex continued his cautious descent, hoping to find some sign of civilization or other markers to help him identify where he had landed. The warm day and unfamiliar surroundings intensified his awareness of the challenges ahead. Despite this, he remained purpose-driven by the need to uncover the secrets this location held.

* * *

Alex followed the slope, carefully picking his way down the rugged terrain. As he descended, the view shifted, revealing a sight at the bottom that took his breath away—a pink lake under a clear blue sky. The water shimmered slightly with an ethereal hue, creating a scene of unusual beauty.

He paused for a moment, taking in the fascinating sight. The vibrant pink of the lake against the azure sky above was mesmerizing, creating an almost otherworldly atmosphere. Alex had never seen anything like it, and the uniqueness of the view made it difficult for him to guess his location.

Curiosity and caution sparked within him in equal measure. He scanned the area, looking for any signs of life or human presence, but the surroundings appeared desolate and untouched. The silence was profound, broken only by the occasional whisper of the wind.

Alex continued his descent, his eyes fixed on the lake. As he drew closer, the intensity of the colour became even more striking. The pink water lapped gently against the rocky shoreline, its surface reflecting the bright sunlight.

He reached the lake's edge and crouched down, dipping his fingers into the water. It felt cool and smooth, the unusual colour still puzzling him. Alex knew he needed to stay vigilant—this place, while beautiful, held an air of mystery and potential danger.

Rising to his feet, he scanned the horizon, searching for clues to help him identify his location. The surrounding terrain was a mix of rocky outcrops and sparse vegetation, with no clear landmarks to guide him.

* * *

Taking out his phone, Alex activated his map application, waiting for it to establish a satellite connection. After a delay, the screen displayed his location near Shiraz, Iran. The detail wasn't great, as he hadn't downloaded maps for areas outside the UK, but it was enough to give him a rough idea of where he was. There can't be too many pink lakes in the world, he thought.

With heightened excitement and apprehension, Alex started recording a panoramic video with his phone, capturing the serene yet alien environment around him. He panned the camera over the pink lake, its vibrant colour standing out against the clear blue sky above. The rocky terrain and scarce vegetation added to the scene's surreal beauty.

As he continued recording, Alex noticed something in the distance—vehicles, partially obscured by the heat ripples from the hot terrain. The sight of them filled him with renewed caution. Human activity nearby could mean potential allies or threats.

He zoomed in with his camera to better see the vehicles. They were difficult to establish but appeared to be military or utility vehicles, their silhouettes distinct against the sandy backdrop of the terrain.

Alex decided to approach cautiously, keeping his distance while he assessed the situation.

The vehicles' presence suggested a nearby settlement or outpost, which might provide valuable information or resources. It also meant Alex needed to avoid drawing unwanted attention to himself or the machine.

He continued documenting his surroundings, making sure to capture every detail. The pink lake, the rocky slopes, the distant vehicles—all were potential clues that could help him piece together the purpose of this location and its significance to Ry-Lan's mission.

* * *

Concerned about being discovered and feeling out of place, Alex decided against venturing closer to the lake or the vehicles. The potential risks of being spotted outweighed the benefits of further exploration. He knew he needed to stay cautious and avoid any unnecessary attention.

Confident that he had gathered sufficient footage for them to review, Alex returned to the security of the machine. The journey up the slope was steady as he constantly scanned the surroundings for any signs of movement or potential threats.

Reaching the alcove where the machine was hidden, Alex took a moment to catch his breath. The rocky walls provided a cooler shadow, a great respite from the open expanse he had just traversed. The path had been steep and uneven, making him hot and sweaty.

The real challenge was the machine's position on a narrow ledge. Earlier, he had let himself down to reach it, but now, reaching the panel to swipe his card was proving to be a struggle. He had to stretch out precariously, his body balanced on the edge as he extended his arm towards the panel. His muscles strained, and he could feel sweat trickling down his back as he exerted himself to maintain his balance.

With great effort, he finally placed the card in the correct location. He let out a sigh of relief as the hatch clicked open, allowing him to climb back into the machine. The exertion had left him feeling drained, but the sense of safety and coolness inside the machine was a great comfort.

Inside, the familiar hum of the machine surrounded him, reassuringly reminding him of its technological prowess. He quickly strapped himself in and activated the controls, setting the coordinates for the journey back to the farm. The machine whirred to life, the lights flickering as it prepared for the jump.

As the world around him blurred and then sharpened into focus, Alex experienced anticipation and relief. He had captured important footage, and now it was time to return and share his findings with Brian. The answers they sought were closer than ever, bringing them nearer to understanding the mystery of Ry-Lan and the machine.

With a final thrum, the machine completed the jump. Alex opened his eyes, and the familiar surroundings of the farm greeted him. He unstrapped himself and stepped out, ready to debrief with Brian and plan their next move.

Sat 27th April 2024

Back at the farm, Alex stepped out of the machine, feeling the warmth of camaraderie as he rejoined Brian. The anticipation was evident in Brian's eyes as he took the SD card out of the bodycam. "You look sweaty. Where did you go? Somewhere hot, I imagine?"

"I think it was to Iran. There was a beautiful pink lake nearby. I expect it will be easy for us to locate it. I got some good footage of it on my phone," Alex said, handing his device to Brian. Do you want to see it?"

Brian's eyes widened as he watched the video, taking in the serene yet alien views. "This is incredible," he murmured, eyes fixed on the screen. "But the vehicles in the distance … any idea who those people are?"

Alex responded as best he could. "No, I don't know. And I didn't want to find out. All the time I was there, I just thought about how difficult it would be to get back here conventionally."

They sat together in Alex's car and watched the rest of the video footage on Brian's laptop screen. The feasibility of travelling to Iran weighed heavily on their minds.

"We'd need visas, flights, accommodations," Brian said, rubbing his temples. "I just don't see how it will be possible."

Alex sighed. "I agree. Even if we were able to sneak over the border, and even if we could get to the location, there's no guarantee we'd be able to stay under the radar, especially with military vehicles in the area. The risk is too high. So, what is the next location on the list?"

Brian pulled up the machine's travel log on the laptop, scrolling through the entries until he found the next significant date. "Here it is—January 2026. We should try this location and see if it's any better. Maybe it'll be more convenient."

Alex felt a ray of hope. "Great. Let's do it!"

Chapter 23

"I'm ready to go again now," Alex declared determinedly.

Brian looked at him, impressed by his spirit. "Are you sure? Do you want a rest first?"

"No, I'm good," Alex replied. "I barely did anything last time. I got all excited for nothing so far."

"OK, if you're sure. Do you need anything else? January might be cold wherever it is you end up."

Alex shook his head, impatience clear in his eyes. "I've got my warm coat. I'll be alright. I'd rather just get on with it. If it's too bad, I can come straight back."

Brian sighed, but he knew better than to argue when Alex was this resolute. "OK, let's do it then."

Brian entered the machine, and in no time, his fingers were deftly navigating through the settings. "This time, you're off to 5th January 2026," he called out while selecting the destination. "It could be anywhere again, so stay alert."

Alex responded quickly, his resolve unwavering. "I'll be careful."

Brian finished programming the destination and stepped back. "Good luck, Alex. Remember, if anything feels off, just come back immediately."

Alex gave him a reassuring smile. "I will. See you soon."

He climbed into the machine, strapping himself in securely. The hatch closed with a finality that echoed through the small space. Alex took a deep breath, feeling the machine's familiar thrum as it powered up. The lights flickered, and the air around him vibrated with energy.

With a final check to ensure everything was in order, Alex initiated the jump.

Mon 5th Jan 2026

The machine's hum faded, signalling its arrival at the new destination. Still strapped securely in his seat, Alex took a deep breath before unfastening the harness. He checked the bodycam, ensuring it was still recording, and then turned on the machine's external video stream. The large monitors changed immediately, revealing the environment outside.

It appeared to be twilight, with the sky painted in soft hues of orange and purple. The machine nestled in a small copse of trees, the dense foliage providing a natural cover. The scene looked peaceful, with no immediate signs of danger.

Alex exited the machine, his boots crunching softly on the leaf-strewn ground. He looked around, taking in the serene surroundings. A short distance away, he spotted a building and decided to investigate.

As he approached, he saw it was a toilet block with "Restrooms" written on it in bold letters. The sight caused him to believe he was in the United States. He continued surveying the area, noticing a road on one side of the building and a golf course on the other. The manicured greens and sand traps stood out against the naturalness of the copse.

On the other side of the road, Alex spotted a vast river, possibly even an estuary, its surface reflecting the dim light of the evening. In the distance, he could make out airport lights on the opposite bank, with the occasional aeroplane coming in.

He took a moment to absorb his surroundings, making mental notes of the landmarks. The presence of the airport could be significant, providing both a clue and a potential transport hub if needed. The peaceful setting belied the magnitude of his mission, but Alex remained vigilant, ready to gather any information to help them understand Ry-Lan's plan.

* * *

Alex took out his phone and checked the map to orient himself. The screen showed he was in Washington, D.C., but the exact location wasn't clear. He heard several police sirens in the distance and figured they must be in the direction of civilization, so he started jogging towards the sound, keeping the river on his left. The freezing air bit his exposed skin, but the running helped him warm up.

As he jogged along the road, he passed several parked cars. He couldn't help but wonder if one of them was what Ry-Lan might have used, but he had no idea which one. Frustration began to creep in as he scanned the area, still searching for any signs that might identify his exact location.

Alex's breath formed small clouds in the chilly air as he picked up the pace, his eyes darting from side to side, looking for anything that could provide a clue. The cars and the surrounding environment offered little information, and his impatience grew with each passing moment.

Occasionally, he passed small clusters of buildings set back from the road. They were mostly anonymous structures—maintenance sheds, small offices, and what looked like abandoned cabins. He slowed slightly, peering into the dimly lit windows, hoping to find some clue, but they revealed nothing of interest.

The cold was starting to penetrate through his thick coat. Despite the running, he could feel the chill settling into his bones. He pressed on, driven by a sense of urgency. The sirens were louder now, and he could see the faint glow of streetlights ahead. Civilization was close.

As he neared the source of the sirens, he noticed a change in the landscape. The trees thinned out, replaced by more manicured lawns and well-lit pathways. He recognised the telltale signs of a park or public recreational area. Seeing more parked cars, these newer and more varied in make and model, confirmed he was getting closer to a more urban setting.

* * *

Alex continued his exploration, the sounds of the city guiding him closer to his goal. After about ten minutes of navigating the increasingly populated area, he finally reached a large building. He approached it cautiously, scanning for any identifying markers. He caught a sign that read, "National Park Service Headquarters Buildings," followed by "1100 Ohio Drive SW."

A sense of satisfaction washed over him. He had finally identified his location accurately. The address confirmed he was in the heart of Washington, D.C., near the Potomac River. He quickly took out his phone and snapped a picture of the sign, ensuring he captured the details clearly.

Feeling a surge of accomplishment, Alex turned around and started returning to the machine. The journey back felt quicker, his steps fuelled by the relief of finding a significant clue. The city noises faded into the background as he retraced his steps along the now-familiar terrain.

As he moved through the park and alongside the river, Alex's mind was racing about what this information could mean. The presence of the National Park Service headquarters suggested that this area held importance, and he wondered how it connected to Ry-Lan's mission. He knew it also represented a realistic destination for him and Brian to reach back in this future timeline.

Alex navigated the last stretch back to the machine with a small burst of acceleration. He knew that every detail he gathered brought them one step closer to understanding the larger puzzle. Reaching the copse where the machine was hidden, he caught his breath and mentally prepared for the jump back.

Climbing into the machine, Alex strapped himself in and triggered the controls, setting the coordinates for the return journey to the farm. The machine jumped to life, the familiar thrum surrounding him as it prepared for the transition.

Sat 27th April 2024

Arriving back at the farm, Alex exited the machine to find Brian waiting for him, his expression eager and curious. Alex quickly recounted his experience, describing the location near the National Park Service Headquarters and the ease with which he identified it.

Brian listened intently, nodding as Alex finished. "A location in the USA in 2026 might be easier for us to get to, even if it means a longer wait," Brian agreed. "Though we shouldn't rule out the Iran one, just in case. We should prepare for both."

He downloaded the video from Alex's bodycam, again transferring the footage to his laptop. They reviewed the video together, with Brian asking a few questions as they watched it.

After reviewing the footage, Brian returned to the machine to check it over before they left. He noticed that the power level was unusually low. After the last trip, it had sat around 72%, and Brian had become accustomed to it dropping by a couple of per cent each trip. But after Alex's trip to Washington, it was down at 23% power remaining.

Brian's face grew tense. "This isn't good, Alex. The machine's power level has dropped from 72% to 23% after your trip to Washington and back."

Alex frowned. "What does that mean for us?"

Brian took a deep breath. "Well, it is the biggest time shift we've done so far. And if the power consumption has the potential to be that high for one round trip, then we might not have enough power for another one. It's a real concern. You might not be able to return from another jump ..."

"So, what do we do?"

Brian looked serious. "I don't think we should use the machine again for the foreseeable future. It's too risky until we figure out why the power dropped so drastically."

Alex seemed a little dejected. "Yes, of course. You're right. We've done enough for today, anyway. It's time to rest and regroup."

They gathered their belongings and left the farm, troubled by the implications of the machine's unexpected power drain. The drive home was filled with cautious discussion, their determination to uncover the truth about Ry-Lan and the machine tempered by the new uncertainty they faced.

As they parted ways, both Alex and Brian felt a heavy responsibility. The next phase of their mission was uncertain, and they knew they had to proceed with extreme caution to avoid further risks.

Chapter 24

Thu 2nd May 2024

To gather more information, Alex focused on Steve, a pivotal figure from the night of the confrontation. Utilizing a blend of digital forensics and old-school detective work, Alex began carefully piecing together Steve's background.

Quickly, he found him on Facebook, though it wasn't too insightful. He clearly liked his lager and had recently returned from a lads' trip to Magaluf. He also seemed to play Sunday league football, though the team didn't appear to be very successful.

To gather more information, Alex contacted Durham CID in Darlington. He made the initial call, explaining the situation and leaving his contact details. Later that afternoon, his phone rang with a return call from Durham CID.

"Good afternoon, Sergeant Harper. This is DI Clarke from Durham CID. I understand you're looking for information on a man named Steve Carlton," came the voice on the other end.

"Yes, thank you for getting back to me. I'm investigating a case that crosses into your jurisdiction and need more information on Steve's background and activities," Alex replied.

"I can't tell you a lot really. As you'll have seen on the PNC, he has no record. He's never been in any kind of trouble. What has he been up to?" DI Clarke asked.

"He was involved in an altercation last week with a person I'm investigating. Do you know where he works, please?" Alex said, giving little away.

"Sure. He works at an abattoir near the airport. I can give you their details if you like," DI Clarke offered.

"That would be great, thank you," Alex agreed.

A short while later, Alex was speaking to the abattoir manager. "Good afternoon. My name is Sergeant Alex Harper, from Helmworth. I'd like to ask you a few questions about one of your employees, Steve Carlton, if I may," Alex said.

"Of course, officer. How can I help? Steve is one of our best workers. He's reliable and hardworking. We've never had any trouble with him," the manager replied.

The manager provided a detailed overview of Steve's work habits and interactions, painting a picture of a diligent and friendly employee. Armed with this information, Alex decided to observe Steve in person. There seemed little point watching him on a workday, so Alex decided to get up early that Saturday to stake out his house.

Sat 4th May 2024

Alex arrived by 6 a.m., and it was fortunate he did so because Steve went out for a run not long after. Alex found it slightly awkward to follow him at a distance, especially as Steve seemed to prefer running down the cycle paths. In the end, Alex decided to head back and wait for him to arrive home. After a 30-minute run, Steve returned home, and Alex settled in for a long wait.

Eventually, Steve left his house around 10 a.m. and drove to a local golf course. Alex again followed at a distance. At the golf course, Steve met a group of men for a round of golf. Alex watched from a discreet distance. Steve seemed relaxed and at ease, laughing and joking with his friends. There was no hint of stress or secrecy in his demeanour.

In the afternoon, Steve and his friends finished their game and headed to the golf course bar for lunch. Alex positioned himself at a table nearby, close enough to overhear snippets of their conversation. They talked about work, sports, and weekend plans—nothing out of the ordinary or suspicious.

The evening took a different turn. After heading home to get changed, Steve walked into the town centre. Alex followed cautiously in his car, keeping a safe distance. Steve moved with a purpose, clearly familiar with the route. The town centre was bustling with activity as people enjoyed their Saturday night out.

Steve entered the Darlington Flyer, where he was clearly a regular, judging by the reaction of the others already there. Alex found a spot at the bar with a clear view of Steve but far enough away to remain unnoticed. Steve ordered a drink and joined a group of men at a table. They laughed and chatted, the atmosphere lively and carefree. Alex observed the interactions, noting Steve's relaxed manner.

As the night progressed, Steve moved to different pubs, socializing and drinking. Alex followed, always at a safe distance. Steve's behaviour remained consistent—friendly and sociable, with no signs of distress or unusual activity. He seemed like any other man enjoying a night out with friends.

The surveillance extended late into the night, with Steve finally leaving the last pub around midnight. He walked home, his steps steady despite the evening's drinks. Alex trailed him, watching as he reached his house safely.

As the weekend drew to a close, Alex felt increased frustration. He had hoped to find some clue, some indication of why Ry-Lan had shown interest in Steve, but nothing was out of the ordinary. Steve's life was as typical as any other, leaving Alex with more questions than answers.

Mon 6th May 2024

Back in Helmworth, the start of the week brought an unexpected and troubling phone call for Alex. As he sat writing up his notes on Steve, his phone rang, displaying Tommy's name on the screen.

"Tommy, what's going on?" Alex asked, concerned.

"Alex, it's bad." Tommy's voice was heavy with despair. "There's been a disease outbreak at a nearby farm. And there's been a case among my sheep, too. The authorities have ordered my entire flock to be culled."

A sinking feeling plunged through Alex's chest. "Oh no, Tommy. I'm so sorry to hear that. How bad is it?"

"It's devastating," Tommy replied, his voice cracking. "I'll lose everything. My whole livelihood will be gone in a matter of days. I don't know what to do."

Tommy's words hit Alex hard. He knew how much the farm meant to Tommy, not just as a source of income but as a way of life. The farm was everything to him.

"Is there anything I can do to help?" Alex asked, feeling helpless but wanting to offer support.

"I don't know. Defra's sending people out. They'll handle the culling and everything, but ... it's just such a blow. I'm not sure how I'll get through this," Tommy said, his predicament evident in every word.

"Listen, Tommy, I know this is devastating, but you're strong. You've got the grit to get through this. Just do what they say and take things one day at a time."

Tommy let out a heavy sigh. "Yeah, I suppose you're right. It's just hard to see the light at the end of the tunnel right now."

"Have they told you about any support? Maybe there are emergency funds or grants you can apply for to help you get back on your feet," Alex suggested, trying to steer the conversation towards practical solutions.

"I'll look into it. Right now, it's just a lot to process. Thanks for listening, Alex. It means a lot," Tommy said, his tone slightly more hopeful.

"Anytime, Tommy. I'm here for you. Call me if you need anything, even if it's just to talk," Alex assured him.

After hanging up, Alex couldn't shake the helplessness that lingered. He knew how much Tommy had invested in the farm, financially and emotionally. Losing the flock was a severe setback, but Alex hoped that with time and support, Tommy would find a way to rebuild.

* * *

Meanwhile at the hospital, Ry-Lan's condition grew increasingly dire. The advanced technological enhancements that had once sustained him appeared now to be failing, causing significant concern among the medical staff. Despite their best efforts to understand and integrate foreign technology, the situation rapidly deteriorated.

The beeping of monitors filled the room, a constant reminder of Ry-Lan's precarious state. Doctors and nurses moved urgently, their faces marked with determination and anxiety. Initially thought to be a breakthrough in Ry-Lan's treatment, the enhancements had become unpredictable and unreliable.

"He's definitely deteriorating," one of the doctors said, frustration evident in his voice. "His enhancements appear to be failing, and we can't seem to keep him stable."

The team huddled together, discussing the best course of action. They decided to revert to more conventional treatments, hoping that traditional medicine could provide some relief while advanced technology could not. Ry-Lan's oxygen levels suffered, requiring a ventilator to help.

The medical staff had marvelled at the sophistication of Ry-Lan's enhancements. The technology was far beyond anything they had encountered, blending seamlessly with his biological systems. Yet, it was clear that even this advanced technology had its limits.

Ry-Lan's breathing was shallow, each breath a struggle. His skin, once a healthy hue, was now pale and clammy. The room filled with the soft hum of machines and the murmurs of the medical team focused entirely on stabilizing their patient.

One of the nurses, a seasoned professional with years of experience, administered injections designed to boost Ry-Lan's immune system and reduce inflammation. She glanced at the monitors, noting a slight improvement in his heart rate.

"He's starting to stabilise," she said, her voice calm but firm.

The head doctor acknowledged her, his forehead wrinkled in concentration. " Let's focus on keeping him comfortable and stable for now. The focus now should be to help him get through the next 48 hours."

As the hours passed, the conventional treatments seemed to provide some temporary relief. Ry-Lan's vitals stabilised slightly, offering a glimmer of hope to his medical team. Yet, the underlying issues with his enhancements remained unresolved, a constant threat to his fragile state.

Sat 11th May 2024

Alex was worried about the machine's security at the farm, especially after the visit from government officials. Determined to protect it, he decided to try to move the machine into one of the nearby barns for safekeeping. He enlisted Tommy's help for the arduous task. The machine was cumbersome, making the move a significant challenge.

They started by carefully planning the operation. Alex inspected the path between the machine's current location and the barn. He knew that the slight decline would aid their efforts. They decided to use Tommy's tractor, a sturdy rope, and a cargo net to manoeuvre the machine. They knew they had to be exceptionally careful, as any mistake could damage the machine.

One bright morning, they began the move. They attached the ropes to the tractor, which Tommy would drive slowly to control the descent. Alex stayed close to the machine, ready to guide and steady it.

As the tractor started, the ropes creaked under the strain, and the machine began to move. The weight was immense, and they had to proceed with painstaking caution. Alex constantly communicated with Tommy, signalling him to adjust the speed and direction.

"Stop!" Alex shouted as the rolling sphere gained momentum. The gentle slope that had seemed so helpful now presented a real challenge as they had no obvious way of stopping the machine.

Fortunately, the machine hit a rut in the ground caused by repeated tractor usage and came to a stop. The men breathed sighs of relief as they released what damage they might have done if the descent had got out of control.

Once again, they started pulling the machine, much more slowly this time. After what felt like an eternity, they finally reached the barn. Tommy swung open the large doors and revealed the spacious interior that would now house the machine. The final challenge was getting the machine inside and positioned correctly. The sphere's smooth and continuous exterior made it difficult to identify the top, though the patterns of the mud and splatter on the machine did help to orient it.

After hours of work, it was finally in place. Exhausted but relieved, they leaned against the barn wall. During this intense labour, Alex couldn't help but notice Tommy's demeanour. The recent outbreak and the loss of his livestock had clearly taken a toll on him. Tommy, usually cheerful, now had worry lines marking his face, and his eyes, once bright with enthusiasm, held a distant, sorrowful look.

"How are you holding up, Tommy?" Alex asked, pausing to catch his breath and check on his friend.

Tommy sighed deeply. "It's been tough, Alex. I feel like I've lost everything. The farm was my life, and now ... I don't know where to start rebuilding."

Alex felt sympathy for his friend. The physical labour had been gruelling, but the emotional drain on Tommy was even more evident. Despite their success in securing the machine, his friend's pain left Alex feeling flat. Alex knew that Tommy's recovery would take time. The emotional and financial blow was significant, and the road ahead would be challenging.

Alex said goodbye to Tommy. He drove along the track to Bingley farm gates and then brought his car to a stop some ten metres from them. The black Audi blocking his way out was all too familiar. And if he needed any confirmation of the driver's identity, he got it when the tall, willowy, grey-haired form of CI West stepped out of the car.

"Sergeant Harper ..." The CI strolled around the Audi to join him, arms folded across her chest. "These updates I keep asking you for that never seem to arrive – I've got fed up with waiting, so I've come to see this mystery object for myself."

Alex's heart rate shot through the roof. How much had she seen? The spot where the machine had lain was remote, but any movement could have been seen with a discerning eye, and the CI certainly had that. How long had she been there? He'd no way of knowing, so he steadied his nerves and went for it:

"It's gone, Ma'am," Alex said as evenly as he could. "That's why I'm here. I was just about to update you. Like you said, it was probably just a prank that went wrong."

"Forget the updates, Sergeant; you're not exactly an expert at them." The CI placed her fingers against her lips and stared out across the farm. "Whereabouts was it?"

Alex raised a hand, fingers indicating into the distance, just hoping she didn't decide to march over and notice any marks leading to the barn. She took a step forward, and then her shoe sunk into the mud. "Ugh! I've left my boots at the station, but I've half a mind to have you drive me closer."

Alex felt her grey eyes studying him. "Still, if it's gone, it's gone. I had it marked down as a prank, and my instincts are seldom wrong." The CI turned away, back to her car. "And the condition of the casualty?"

"Still unconscious, Ma'am, I'm afraid. Unresponsive. But I'll …"

"Keep me updated. Yes, I know, Sergeant. I live in hope."

And with that, the CI drove away, and Alex breathed again.

Wed 15th May

As time slipped by and concern for Ry-Lan's health grew, Alex and Brian became increasingly focused on the feasibility of a trip to Iran in October. They met at Alex's house, the dining table covered with maps, information from the Foreign, Commonwealth and Development Office, and a laptop open to various relevant sites.

"Ry-Lan's condition is deteriorating faster than we anticipated," Brian said, his tone urgent. "If there's any chance we can help him by understanding what's happening in Iran, we need to consider it seriously."

"Agreed. But getting to Iran is no small feat, especially with the current geopolitical climate. We would need to plan this thoroughly."

They began by exploring various travel options. There were no direct flights to Iran, though changing in Turkey or Dubai was possible. However, a Briton arriving in Tehran by plane would attract a lot of unwanted attention. They considered flying into a neighbouring country and then crossing the border by land, but that presented its own set of challenges, including increased scrutiny and potential delays.

"I just can't see how we could travel there legally," Brian pointed out, scrolling through the FCDO website. "We'd never get a visa, and it's too high profile. Could we get across the border from Turkey or catch a boat from Dubai?"

"I don't think that's realistic," Alex countered. "We don't know anyone there, and we would be at the mercy of criminals."

They spent hours discussing the problem, each time drawing a blank.

"I just don't think Ry-Lan will last long enough to wait for us to go to Washington instead," Alex said. "His life is hanging by a thread already."

By the end of it, they were thoroughly depressed. There seemed to be no route forward, though they were still not ready to give up.

Mon 3rd June

The monotony of preparation and waiting was suddenly broken one evening by an unexpected knock on Alex's door. Startled, Alex opened it, and to his shock and overwhelming joy stood his brother, Mark.

"Mark!" Alex exclaimed, full of disbelief and happiness. He pulled Mark into a tight embrace, relief washing over him. "I can't believe you're here."

Mark returned the embrace, though with less intensity. "Hey, Alex," he said, a smile on his lips.

Pulling back, Alex beamed at his brother. "Come in, come in!" He ushered Mark inside, his mind flooded with a thousand questions but choosing to savour the moment of reunion first. "You have no idea how good it is to see you."

Mark stepped inside, glancing around Alex's home as if seeing it for the first time. "It's good to see you too," he said, his voice carrying cautious excitement. "We have so much to catch up on."

They were quiet and at ease for a while, but the heaviness of the previous months lingered in the atmosphere. Alex was bursting with happiness and relief, the presence of his brother a balm to his frayed nerves. He wanted to savour every second, to hold onto this moment of unexpected joy.

Mark seemed a bit more reserved but not unenthusiastic. He looked around the room, his eyes landing on familiar items. "It's been a while," he finally said with a small smile.

"When did you get back?"

"Saturday morning. I spent a couple of days with Kate and Ethan. We had a lot of catching up to do. And then I wanted to come and see you," Mark replied.

Finally, unable to contain his curiosity any longer, Alex looked at Mark with hope and anticipation. "Tell me everything," he said softly, his voice conveying the months of worry and uncertainty.

Mark met his brother's gaze, and his expression brightened for the first time that evening. He took a deep breath, ready to share the story of his disappearance and the journey that had brought him back to Alex's doorstep.

Chapter 25

Alex moved closer, his eyes gleaming with curiosity. "So, then. Start at the beginning. What happened after I phoned you?"

Mark took a deep breath, his tired eyes reflecting the toil of his experiences. "Well, after we spoke, I really didn't know what to think. It just all sounded so unbelievable. But then COVID-19 happened, just like you said it would."

Alex's heart swelled with pride and relief. "I was so worried you wouldn't believe me."

"To be honest, at first, I didn't," Mark admitted with a small chuckle. "But when the Boris thing happened, I knew you were telling the truth. It was eerie, watching everything unfold exactly as you described. That prophecy gave me the confidence to believe you."

Mark continued, "The pandemic was such a crazy time. I wasn't worried, though. How could I be? I already knew that I was going to survive it. That made such a huge difference. In hindsight, I do wish I'd asked more questions, though. It could have been useful to know more in advance."

"So, what happened next?" Alex asked eagerly.

Mark reflected, his expression growing more serious. "During the pandemic, we were stationed near Manchester, helping with the testing efforts. But wait, you know this already, don't you? We used to talk on Zoom regularly during that time."

"Yes, but you didn't let on that you'd been visited by a future me," Alex reminded him.

"Yeah, I mean no, well, I couldn't. Could I?"

"No, of course not. What happened next?"

"Well, I started saving money, like big time. I got a lot of money." Mark smiled as he thought about what he was saying. "And then I thought, I should prepare for the future, for my disappearance. So, I did. We had a deployment in Germany. When I finished there, I took a few weeks off and travelled to eastern Turkey, to a place called Van. And then, I went down to the border region near Iraq and toured the area. And made a few friends …"

Mark stopped for a drink. "I also found a place up in the mountains near Çatak. I thought it would make a good hideout. And the local Agha, Masoud, seemed agreeable, so I paid him to keep the place for me, ready to escape. He knew some useful people, too.

"Then I came back to the UK for a while and waited," Mark continued. "Eventually, we were sent to Iraq, and I knew what was coming, of course. Masoud helped to hook me up with some of his friends, and one time when I was out on manoeuvres with another guy from our unit, they staged an abduction. It was pretty intense, actually. They hid us for a couple of days, then let my mate go and took me across the border. I think they might even have demanded a ransom for me to the army, but good luck with that!"

Alex listened in rapt attention. "Go on."

"So, I made my way back up to my place in the mountains and waited it out. Masoud and his family looked after me and supplied me with everything I needed."

"Didn't you go out at all?"

"Yeah, a bit. I grew my beard and shaved my head. I also picked up the language pretty quickly. I'd learned a bit of Kurdish while in the army, so it wasn't completely new to me."

"Masoud took me out fishing with some of his sons too, quite often," Mark reminisced. "It was pretty cold in winter, though. We didn't get out much then. One year, it snowed really bad. I made some homemade skis and went out on them. You'd have loved it there."

Alex enjoyed seeing Mark smile and laugh again. He had really missed him. "I am so pleased to see you again."

Mark smiled though his eyes held traces of his ordeal. "Yes, me too."

"So, how did you get back home?"

"Well, as we got closer to the time you had said, I started to make plans. Masoud helped me get a ride west to Antep. Then I walked into a police station there and told them I'd been held hostage and escaped. I said the Kurds had taken me into Syria and kept me there for over two years. I told them I'd escaped across the border and wanted to get home."

"And they believed you?"

"Yes, they were really kind. They took me to the British embassy and brought in army intelligence to talk to me. They got me flown back to England and transferred to Headley Court in Surrey. It was a bit more difficult with the army, but I already had my story straight in my head and just stuck to it religiously."

"Did they tell Kate you were back?"

"Sure, they were pretty good about it all. They let her come up and see me there as well. And I was back home within about a week anyway."

"How did Kate take it all? It must have been awful for her," Alex began. "I really tried hard to help her while you were gone. Truly, I did. But she wouldn't let me. We used to be so close. I thought she'd be happy to see me ... Well, maybe not 'happy', but I could still help."

Mark sighed, setting his cup down on the table and looking away for a moment before meeting Alex's gaze. "I know, Alex. She told me you tried to help."

The way Mark said it made Alex uneasy, as if an unspoken tension lingered in the air. "She told you ...?" Alex trailed off, hoping Mark would clarify.

Mark hesitated, then continued, "Yes, I was in touch with her while I was away. She even came to visit me a few times in Turkey. It was complicated, Alex. You have no idea how difficult it was."

The revelation hit Alex hard. He sat back in his chair, processing the information. "I had no idea she visited you. I thought it was too risky for both of you."

Mark rubbed his head, looking weary. "We had to take the risk. It was the only way to keep our family together. She was my lifeline, Alex. Those visits, those calls ... they kept me going. But it wasn't easy. Every time she left, it felt like I was being torn apart all over again."

Alex's mind raced with the implications. "I can't even imagine what you went through. I only said what I did because I was worried about the consequences. I was scared something might happen to either of you. But now that you're here and safe, it seems like everything turned out OK."

Mark's expression softened slightly. "I know you were trying to help, and I appreciate that. It's just ... things are complicated. There were times when I thought I wouldn't make it, and she was dealing with so much on her own back here."

Alex looked down at his cup, feeling a pang of guilt. "Like what? I know should have been there more for her while you were away. I tried. Maybe I should have done more."

"You did what you thought was best," Mark said, his tone revealing apology and frustration. "We both did. It's just ... we've all been through a lot, and we're still figuring things out. But we'll get there."

Alex reflected on Mark's words. He felt glad that despite the tension, they were both committed to moving forward and repairing any rifts, but something still bugged him. "We will," Alex said at length. "And I'm here for you, whatever you need."

A small smile played out on Mark's lips, but his eyes relayed a different story. Alex couldn't tell what it was, but the way his brother avoided his gaze told him that Mark was holding something back. "What aren't you telling me, Mark?"

Mark met Alex's stare, if only for a second, and then he let out a heavy breath. "I'm sorry, Alex, I should have told you."

"Come on, Mark," Alex urged, leaning forward. "Don't keep it bottled up. It can't be..."

"She resents you for making me leave," Mark interrupted him with a sigh.

Alex shook his head. "I still don't understand. She's been off with me for such a long time." Alex paused, swept a hand across his face in frustration, his lips forming a perfect 'O'. He slapped a hand on the table. "She's known longer than I have."

Mark nodded. "Two years is a long time." He pressed his palms together, elbows on the table. "I should have also told you that Kate's kept up her friendship with Amy. Your ex doesn't paint a rosy picture of you it seems, from the little Kate's told me, but she knows it's only one side of the story. She doesn't hold that against you. It's just, you know..."

"Well, I do now." Alex bit his lip. "Thanks for enlightening me."

Kate had kept her resentment bottled up for quite some while. Alex shook his head and sighed. He might have known. And the truth was, as far as Amy was concerned, she'd always been demanding and hard work. With his profession came a responsibility to his employers that sometimes left Amy feeling neglected. She never was, not in his book, but that was how she no doubt saw it and conveyed the same to Kate.

Now, he knew, but there was no sense in blaming either Mark or Kate. It was just the way things were.

The brothers sat silently for a moment, feeling the heaviness of their shared experiences. The path ahead was still uncertain, but despite what Alex had just been told, they would face it as a family. Though tested and strained, the bond between them had not been broken. Perhaps, Alex thought, a quiet word with Kate would suffice and create a new beginning, one they could welcome with open hearts.

* * *

As the evening wore on, the conversation began to shift. The initial flood of emotions from their reunion started to ebb, giving way to curiosity and intrigue. Mark began pacing thoughtfully.

"You know, Alex," he began, his tone lighter, "all this talk about the past and the future ... it's got me thinking. About this time travel ... When we last spoke, it sounded insane, but now, after everything that's happened, I'm genuinely curious. How did you manage it?"

Alex's eyes lit up at the question, his passion for the subject evident. "It's a long story, Mark. But it's real. The machine, time travel ... it's all real." Alex proceeded to explain to Mark how Ry-Lan's machine first appeared, as well as the hospital and all that had ensued.

Mark sat close to Alex. "Can you show me the machine? Can you explain how it works?"

Alex smiled. "Of course. I'll show you the machine tomorrow and explain how it functions. Well, I'll tell you what I know anyway. Brian will be able to explain it better."

"Who is Brian?" Mark asked.

"Brian's a friend of mine. He's been with me every step of the way, helping me figure out how the machine works and what we can do with it," Alex explained.

"I can't wait to see it. You've always been the one with the crazy ideas, Alex, but I never imagined something like this."

Alex chuckled, a sense of camaraderie warming his heart. "Yeah, it's definitely out there. But it's also the most incredible thing I've ever experienced. And it's changed everything."

Mark's eyes widened. "And all this time, I thought I was the one having adventures. You've been out there, travelling through time."

Alex grinned. "It's been quite the journey. But seeing you here, safe and sound makes it all worth it. I can't wait to show you the machine tomorrow. You'll finally get to see what all the fuss is about."

Mark smiled, excitement and disbelief on his face. "I'm looking forward to it. And Alex ... thank you. For saving my life. For everything."

Alex reached over, giving his brother's shoulder a reassuring squeeze. "We've been through a lot, Mark. But we're still here, still fighting. And now, we have even more to look forward to."

As the night drew to a close, Mark stood up, preparing to leave. "I'll see you tomorrow then. Bright and early?"

"Bright and early," Alex agreed, walking him to the door. "Goodnight, Mark."

"Goodnight, Alex," Mark replied, stepping out into the cool night air.

After Mark left, Alex felt a mix of emotions swirling inside him. He pulled out his phone and texted Brian: *Call me!*

There was no immediate reply, but Alex understood. It was late, and Brian was probably asleep. He put his phone down, contentment settling over him. Tomorrow would bring new adventures and the promise of sharing his incredible journey with his brother. As he prepared for bed, he felt renewed hope and excitement for the future.

Chapter 26

Tue 4th June

Alex was already up and having breakfast when his phone rang. Seeing Brian's name on the screen, he quickly answered, anticipating Brian's reaction to the news.

"Morning, Brian," Alex greeted, his voice bright.

"Morning, Alex. Just catching up. You wanted me to call?" Brian's tone was casual, unaware of the surprise awaiting him.

"Brian, you're not going to believe this, but Mark showed up on my doorstep yesterday," Alex said, unable to contain his excitement.

There was a brief pause before Brian replied, "What? Mark's back? How is he? What happened?"

"Yeah, he's back," Alex confirmed. "He's doing alright, considering everything. We spent the whole evening catching up. It's been surreal."

"That's amazing news," Brian said, his tone softening with relief. "So, what's the plan now?"

"Well, I told him about the time travel stuff, and he's really curious. He wants to see the machine. I was thinking of taking him to the farm today," Alex explained.

Brian hesitated for a moment. "I understand your excitement, Alex, but are you sure about this? Involving him so quickly could be a bit too much. Maybe we should take it slower?"

"I get your concern, Brian, but Mark's been through a lot. I think he can handle it," Alex reassured him. "Besides, seeing the machine might help him understand everything better."

"I understand, but do you mind if I come too," Brian said cautiously. "It might take me a bit longer to get there, but I'll come as soon as I can. We still need to be careful."

"Oh, yeah. For sure," Alex agreed. "I've told him all about you. I'd like you both to meet as well. Just come as quickly as you can, please."

"Alright, I'll get there as soon as possible," Brian said carefully. "Take it slow with Mark, though, right?"

"Will do, Brian. Thanks," Alex said, feeling that Brian would approve of his brother once they met. "See you soon."

Alex put his phone down and finished his breakfast, buzzing with anticipation but nervous as well.

With a final glance around his home, Alex grabbed his keys and headed out, ready to embark on this new chapter with his brother and friend by his side.

* * *

Alex pulled up to Mark's house, anticipation and trepidation lingering. He parked his car and trod the familiar path to the front door. Taking a deep breath, he knocked firmly, the sound echoing slightly in the quiet morning.

After a moment, the door opened to reveal Mark's wife, Kate. Her expression was carefully neutral, her eyes reflecting a coolness he now partly understood. She wasn't outright rude, but the warmth that once defined their relationship was notably absent.

"Morning, Kate," Alex greeted, trying to keep his tone light and friendly.

"Morning, Alex," Kate replied, polite but distant. She stepped aside to let him in, avoiding any unnecessary small talk.

Alex entered the house, glancing around at the familiar surroundings. "Is Mark ready?"

"He's just finishing up," Kate said, motioning towards the living room. "You can wait in there if you like."

Alex strolled to the living room, trying to ignore the tension in the air. He could hear Mark moving around upstairs, the sound of footsteps a reassuring reminder of his brother's presence.

Kate followed him into the living room but remained standing. "Where are you going?" she asked, her tone still reserved.

"There's something I need to show Mark," Alex replied, choosing his words carefully. "We won't be too long. Maybe a couple of hours."

Kate's eyes narrowed slightly, but she didn't press for details. Instead, she just exhaled loudly through her nose and then walked out. Alex watched her go, feeling the urge to call her back. He wanted to bring up the subject of Mark and him going away, but now wasn't the time. Besides, he couldn't adequately explain it.

Just then, Mark appeared at the top of the stairs with a small smile. "Ready to go?"

"Yeah, let's do this," Alex replied, springing up.

Mark gave Kate a quick kiss on the cheek. "I'll be back soon. Don't worry."

Kate's eyes softened as she looked at her husband. "Alright. Take care."

Alex and Mark headed out to the car, the friction from moments before lingering slightly but overshadowed by the expectation of the day's events. As they drove away from the house, Alex glanced over at Mark.

"Sorry about Kate," Mark said, sensing his brother's unease, but at least you've an inkling of why she's like that with you."

"I get it," Alex replied, determined to focus on the matter at hand. "Let's focus on today. I think you're going to find this really fascinating."

Mark nodded, a flicker of excitement in his eyes. "I'm ready, Alex. Let's do it."

* * *

The drive to the farm involved small talk, a way to keep the nerves at bay. As they approached the secluded location, Alex felt his excitement building. He was eager to share this part of his life with Mark, to show him the machine that had changed everything.

Arriving at the farm, Alex parked near the barn that contained the machine. The structure was unassuming, blending in with the rural surroundings, yet safe enough to protect the secret within.

"Welcome to our little hideaway," Alex said, leading Mark towards the structure. He unlocked the barn door and swung it open, revealing the machine inside.

Mark stepped in, his eyes widening as he took in the sight. "Wow, this is ... incredible. It looks so advanced, almost alien."

"Yes, it is. You should see it in the sunlight, though. It really is very impressive," Alex replied with a grin. "We've been careful to keep it hidden and protected. Brian and I have been working on understanding it and using it responsibly."

As they stood before the machine, Alex began to explain their plans. "We've been discussing a potential trip to Iran in October this year. The idea is to meet Ry-Lan there and speak to him when he arrives using this machine. But if that doesn't pan out, our fallback plan is to travel to Washington, D.C., in 2026. But ideally, we don't want to wait that long. Currently, Ry-Lan is in hospital, and we're worried about him. So, we're trying to think if there is a way to get to the Iran location in time."

Mark listened intently, nodding as he processed the information. "I have to say, Alex, this is way beyond anything I ever imagined. I think I can help, though. My time in Turkey taught me a lot, and I picked up some useful language skills. I can speak Kurdish pretty well, and I know people down that way. I could go for us."

Alex was grateful for the offer but felt protective concern. "Mark, I really appreciate that. But you've only just got back. We all went through so much to get you here safely. We can't risk it all again by sending you to Iran."

Mark grasped the seriousness of it all. "I get it, Alex. But I want to help. You've already done so much for me. Let me be there for you this time. I can do this."

Alex sighed. "We'll think about it, Mark. For now, let's focus on what we can do here. We have time to plan and prepare. And having you here, offering your support, means a lot to me."

Alex felt reassured. Sharing this moment with his brother, knowing they were in this together, gave him a renewed sense of purpose.

They stood side by side, contemplating the machine and the future adventures it held, ready to face whatever challenges lay ahead.

* * *

Brian arrived at the farm mid-morning, pulling up beside Alex's car. He stepped out, stretched his legs, and strode towards the barn. Spotting Alex and Mark near the entrance, he approached with a smile but with a hint of curiosity in his eyes.

"Morning, Alex. Ah, you must be Mark," Brian said, extending a hand. "I've heard a lot about you. I'm Brian."

Mark shook Brian's hand firmly. "Good to meet you too, Brian. Thanks for everything you've done for Alex."

"Likewise," Brian replied, though he couldn't help but notice Mark's military bearing, the sharpness in his movements, and the directness in his gaze. But Mark's remark on behalf of Alex struck him as being a touch overbearing, brotherly concern probably, though Brian stored it for future reference. "Alex tells me you're keen to see the machine."

Mark was eager. "Absolutely. Alex has told me some incredible things. I'm eager to learn more and see it in action."

Brian's smile tightened slightly. "Well, it's important to understand the machine fully before we start making any plans. There's a lot at stake."

Alex sensed the tension and intervened. "Let's go inside, and I'll show you both around."

They entered the barn, and Brian went to the lockbox where they kept the access card. He shielded the keypad while he entered the code.

Mark didn't notice. He was too excited about seeing the machine. "This is fantastic. With my skills and experience, I could be a real asset, especially for a trip to Iran."

Brian frowned slightly and shared a glance with Alex. "There are significant risks involved. We need to be cautious."

Mark bristled at Brian's tone. "I understand the risks, Brian. I'm more capable of handling them than Alex is."

Brian's eyes narrowed slightly. "Capability isn't just about individual skills, Mark. It's about teamwork and understanding the nuances of the mission. We've been working on this for a while."

Mark crossed his arms, a defensive edge in his voice. "I've been in plenty of high-risk situations. I know how to handle myself. Besides, I have contacts and language skills that could be crucial."

Brian seemed surprised. "Contacts? What kind of contacts?"

Mark hesitated, then shrugged. "People I've met during my time in Turkey. Some of them could help us navigate into Iran."

Brian's frown deepened. "That's precisely why we need to be careful. We can't just rely on acquaintances that we barely know. There's too much at stake. The machine could fall into the wrong hands."

Mark's frustration boiled over. "Look, I've been out there, risking my life. I know what it takes to survive. I can handle it better than Alex can."

Alex's face darkened; his brother's impetuosity was showing through. "Mark, that's not fair. We've been managing fine without you. Do you have any idea what we've been through to get this far? Your experience could be valuable, but you can't just assume you know better."

Mark kept going. "I'm not saying you haven't done a good job. But you know my background. You know I can handle pressure and make quick decisions in the field."

Alex shook his head, anger and hurt in his eyes. "You think we don't handle pressure here? Every day is a challenge, and we've managed. And let's not forget, you've been seeing your wife while you were in Turkey, so it's not as if you handled it alone."

The atmosphere grew tense, the silence thickening. Brian cleared his throat. "We need to make decisions based on what's best for everyone, not just individual capabilities, so let's leave it at that."

"Fair enough. If that's how you want it, suit yourselves," and with that said, Mark stomped off towards Alex's car.

They barely spoke on the ride home.

Chapter 27

Wed 5th June

The next day, Alex called at Mark's house while on duty, taking advantage of a quiet afternoon and hoping to clear the air a little with his brother. Mark welcomed him in, having seemingly cooled down, and they settled in the living room, the atmosphere initially casual. Mark had already opened a beer and offered one to Alex, too.

"No, thanks. I'm on duty. I just came to see how you've been settling back in."

Mark shrugged. "It's been a bit of an adjustment, but we're getting there. Kate and Ethan are glad to have me back."

"I bet. It must be good to be home."

Mark gave a small smile. "Yeah, it is. What about you? How's your job?"

Alex sighed. "Same old, really. Nothing much happens unless you count the machine, of course. So, what are your plans for the next few weeks?"

Mark glanced away, hesitating before he answered. "We're off to Orlando for a month."

"Orlando? That sounds ... expensive. How can you afford that?"

Mark's hesitation grew more pronounced. "Well, I've been ... lucky."

Alex sensed there was more to the story. "Lucky? How so?"

Mark sighed, clearly reluctant to divulge his secret. "You know. I put some of the information you gave me to good use. And it paid well."

Alex's eyes narrowed. "What do you mean, 'put the information to good use'?"

Mark shifted uncomfortably and looked away. "About the football and the elections. I placed a few bets and won big."

Alex's expression darkened. "You used the information I gave you to gamble?"

Mark tried to downplay it. "It's not really gambling if you already know the outcome, right? It was a sure thing."

Alex's voice was low and intense. "What the hell, Mark! That's not why I gave you that information."

Mark became defensive. "I don't see what the problem is. It's not like it hurt anyone. Besides, how do you think I was supposed to survive for two years in the mountains? I did what I had to do. And I still have a bit left over. It's only fair. I haven't got a job now, thanks to you."

Alex shook his head, frustration evident. "That's not what this is about. This machine isn't a get-rich-quick scheme. It's dangerous, and we have to be responsible. We mustn't draw attention to ourselves."

Mark sighed. "Alright, alright, I get it. I won't do it again."

Alex rolled his eyes, unable to disguise his disappointment. "I hope you mean that. Because if you don't, you'll be putting us all at risk."

Mark tried to reach out. "Alex, come on. Let's not blow this out of proportion."

Alex stood up, glancing at his watch. "I've got to get back to work now. Enjoy your trip to Orlando. We'll talk when you get back."

Mark watched as Alex left, his brother's words still hanging in the air. The reunion had been far from what Alex had hoped for, leaving him frustrated and disheartened.

Tue 11th June

Days later, Alex was in the middle of his shift at the police station when his phone rang. The caller ID showed the hospital's number. He had a feeling he was not going to like this call.

"Hello, Sergeant Harper speaking."

"Hello, officer. This is Dr Patel from the hospital. I'm calling about Ry-Lan. I'm afraid his condition has deteriorated critically."

Alex's heart sank. "What do you mean? What happened?"

Dr Patel's voice was calm but urgent. "His implants, which had previously stabilised him, are now failing. We weren't sure if you wanted to know."

"I'll be there right away," Alex replied, his brain whirling as he hung up. He quickly informed his supervisor of the emergency and left the station.

The drive to the hospital felt like an eternity, each minute stretched by mental torture. Alex's thoughts were a whirlwind of worry and fear. When he finally arrived, he rushed through the hospital corridors to Ry-Lan's room.

Dr Patel met him outside the room, her expression grave. "Hello, officer. As I said on the phone, Ry-Lan is in a critical condition. We've tried everything we can to stabilise him but without success."

Alex looked through the window at Ry-Lan, who lay motionless on the bed. "What can we do?" he asked desperately.

Dr Patel shook her head. "We're reverting to conventional treatments but can only do so much. His body appears to be rejecting the implants."

Alex felt a lump form in his throat. "Can I go in and see him?"

"Of course," Dr Patel said, stepping aside to let him enter the room.

Alex approached Ry-Lan's bedside, his heart heavy with worry. He gently placed a hand on Ry-Lan's shoulder. "Hang in there, buddy. The doctors are doing everything they can."

As the medical staff continued their efforts, Alex stood by, feeling helpless. The fear of losing Ry-Lan gnawed at him, and he silently hoped for a miracle. Sounds of machines and hushed voices filled the room, reminders of Ry-Lan's precarious condition.

Time seemed to stretch on endlessly as Alex watched, waiting for any improvement. But the reality of Ry-Lan's situation was undeniable. It was dire, and all Alex could do was offer what support he could in the face of an uncertain outcome.

* * *

The doctors decided that surgery was the only option left. They prepped Ry-Lan for the operation, aiming to remove the malfunctioning implants causing his body to fail. Alex watched helplessly as they wheeled Ry-Lan's bed into the operating theatre, a sense of dread settling deep in his stomach.

The waiting room was cold and sterile, amplifying Alex's anxiety. He paced back and forth, glancing at the clock every few minutes. Each tick seemed to echo in the silence, a static warning of precious time slipping away.

An hour passed, each minute stretching longer than the last. Finally, Dr Patel emerged from the operating room, her face solemn. Alex's heart sank at the sight of her expression.

"I'm sorry, officer," she began, her voice gentle yet heavy with sorrow. "We did everything we could, but Ry-Lan didn't make it through the surgery."

The words hit Alex like a physical blow. He felt his legs give way and sank into a nearby chair, struggling to process the loss. Tears welled up in his eyes, and a profound sense of grief and isolation enveloped him.

He stayed in the waiting room for what felt like an eternity, grappling with the reality of Ry-Lan's death. The medical staff moved around him, their quiet conversations a distant hum in his ears.

Overwhelmed with emotion, Alex reached for his phone and called Brian. The line rang twice before Brian picked up.

"Alex? What's up?" Brian's voice was calm, though his worry was obvious.

"It's Ry-Lan," Alex managed to say, his voice choked with tears. "He's gone, Brian. He's dead."

Brian was silent for a moment, absorbing the news. "I'm so sorry, Alex. I know how much he meant to you."

The floodgates opened, and Alex's grief poured out. "It's not fair, Brian. We tried so hard, and now he's gone. What do we do?"

Brian's steady presence on the other end of the line provided a small measure of comfort. "I know it's hard, Alex. But you're not alone. We'll get through this together."

Alex took a shaky breath, trying to steady himself. "I just ... I can't believe he's really gone."

"Take your time. It's okay to feel this way," Brian assured him. "Ry-Lan was important to both of us."

As Alex continued talking, relief slowly started seeping in. Brian's loyalty and support were unwavering, a steady anchor in the storm of his grief. For the first time in what felt like an eternity, Alex leant on his friend, recognizing the depth of their bond.

"Thank you, Brian," Alex said quietly. "I don't know what I'd do without you."

Brian's response was simple but heartfelt. "We're in this together, Alex. Always."

Wed 12th June

Alex remained consumed by a profound sense of regret the next day. He'd been given time off work for compassionate reasons, and for the last few hours, he'd been sitting in his small, dimly lit living room, watching the video of Ry-Lan from the stadium car park over and over, when Brian called him.

"How are you doing, Alex?" Brian asked. "Is there anything I can do to help?"

"I keep thinking, Brian," Alex ignored his friend's question, "that we failed him. Ry-Lan seemed to know and trust me somehow, and we couldn't save him. Is there any point in still going to Iran or Washington? Do you think we would be able to warn him, like we did to Mark? Would it bring him back to life? Or perhaps it would mean that he never even came here in the first place, and then what would happen?"

Brian listened patiently to him. "I get it, Alex. It's hard not to feel that way. But we did everything we could with the knowledge we had. Sometimes, despite our best efforts, things don't go as we hoped."

Alex still wanted to talk about the planned trips. "But what's the point of these missions if we can't make a meaningful difference? What if we're just chasing shadows?"

Brian sighed. "We have to believe that what we're doing matters. Maybe we couldn't save Ry-Lan, but that doesn't mean we won't make a difference in the future. We owe it to him to keep trying."

Alex accepted this, though his heart still felt heavy. "I just don't want to go through this again, Brian. The thought of losing someone else..."

"I know. But giving up now won't change what happened. If anything, it'll make Ry-Lan's sacrifice meaningless. We have to keep going for his sake."

Brian was glad that Alex had called. He wanted to tell Alex about an idea he'd had. "Listen. About the plan. I've been thinking about it, and I believe there is a way we can do it without waiting."

"Go on."

"Well, do you remember your first two jumps and how, by accident, you ended up at the same coordinates that Ry-Lan used and how the machine adjusted the jump slightly to allow it to work? Maybe we can use that phenomenon to our advantage."

Alex listened intently. "What do you mean?"

"Well, we've been travelling to the same moment that Ry-Lan has just left, his exit coordinates. But if we select the jump coordinates as he did, his entry coordinates, then we might be able to arrive at the same time he does in Washington. I say Washington because I think it would be much better to meet up with him there rather than try to meet him in Iran."

The idea rejuvenated Alex. "That's brilliant! If we can meet Ry-Lan in Washington, we can confront him and maybe help him while it's still possible. We may still yet be able to save his life."

Brian's enthusiasm was growing, too. "Exactly. We must still be careful, but I think it will work."

"What about the power level, though? I thought we couldn't use the machine anymore in case I couldn't get back home."

"Yeah, about that," Brian paused. "I still don't understand what happened yet, but the machine's history shows that the last jump consumed the normal amount of power. Something else must have drained it. It wasn't your journey that did it."

Alex bit his lip, his enthusiasm rekindled. "I really want to do this. Can we do it today?"

"No, I can't today," Brian said, checking his calendar. "I can be available to come over the day after tomorrow. And we can talk again tomorrow to finalise our plans and ensure everything is ready."

Alex agreed, his recent despair replaced by newfound determination. "Perfect. I'm happy to wait. We'll get everything sorted, and then we'll go."

Chapter 28

<u>Fri 14th June</u>

The early morning sun cast long shadows over Bingley farm as Alex drove up the familiar dirt path, the air thick with anticipation. When he arrived, he noticed that Tommy was notably absent, a reminder of the recent hardships that had befallen the farm.

Brian was already there, his car parked beside the barn. He was busy setting up the machine, his movements precise and methodical.

Alex joined him. "Morning, Brian," Alex greeted, his voice steady but laced with a hint of nervousness.

Alex watched as Brian selected the coordinates to match Ry-Lan's previous arrival in Washington. The machine's complex interface never ceased to amaze him.

"Are we sure about this?" Alex asked uncertainly. "What if something goes wrong?"

Brian paused, turning to face Alex. "We've done our homework, Alex. We've reviewed the data from your previous jumps and Ry-Lan's patterns. This is our best shot at aligning with his arrival. We need to trust the plan."

Alex took a deep breath, trying to calm his racing thoughts. "You're right. We have to try."

Brian continued his adjustments, the machine humming as it powered up. The air inside the barn seemed to thrum with energy, fear, and hope. Alex, dressed for the winter conditions in Washington, busied himself by checking his equipment, ensuring his preparedness for whatever awaited them.

"Remember," Brian said, his voice breaking the silence, "you will need to be fairly quick. Check the cameras as normal and then go straight to see Ry-Lan. If you delay, then he may have already left. But also, don't take risks. We can always jump there again if needed."

Alex glanced at Brian worriedly. "I'm really nervous, Brian. There's a lot resting on this."

With the final preparations complete, Brian stepped back from the machine resolutely. "Alright, Alex. This is it. Are you ready?"

Alex looked at the machine, then back at Brian. "Ready as I'll ever be."

Before Alex could enter the machine, Brian thoroughly checked the machine's interior, making sure that the seat and harness were secure. He also made sure that Alex's bodycam was functioning. "Just making sure you're set," Brian said reassuringly.

Alex appreciated the gesture, Brian's thoroughness having boosted his confidence. "Thanks, Brian. It means a lot."

As the machine's hum grew louder, so Alex's resolve strengthened. They had come too far to turn back now. With Brian's support, he felt re-energized. This journey was about more than just meeting Ry-Lan; it was about making a difference, no matter how daunting the path ahead might be.

Tue 15th October 2024

The familiar hum of the time machine intensified, culminating in a final thud as it completed the jump. Alex took a deep breath, his heart pounding with anticipation. He unstrapped himself, adjusted his coat, and ensured his gloves and hat were secure. After checking his bodycam again, he changed the monitor inside the machine to camera mode, ready to assess his surroundings.

The screens revealed Ry-Lan's machine positioned close by, about ten metres ahead, its sleek, metallic surface gleaming in the daylight.

Alex's machine had landed behind Ry-Lan's, providing a good vantage point for observation. He took a moment to steady himself, ensuring all his equipment was in place. The scene was quiet, save for the occasional sway of the nearby trees in the breeze.

With a final deep breath, Alex exited the machine. The air was cold, but the sun provided some small respite. He moved cautiously towards Ry-Lan's machine, each step deliberate and measured. His footsteps were soft on the ground, barely making a sound as he advanced.

As he drew nearer, Alex spotted movement. Ry-Lan exited his machine, scanning the surroundings vigilantly. His figure was more distinct in this setting, the daylight casting a clear view of his form and features.

* * *

Alex's presence clearly surprised Ry-Lan, who hurried over with an intense look of curiosity and concern. Ry-Lan spoke rapidly in his own language, his tone suggesting urgency and confusion.

Alex raised his hands in a calming gesture. "I'm sorry, I don't understand," he said, reaching into his pocket to pull out his phone. He fumbled with the translation app, hoping to bridge the communication gap.

Ry-Lan watched him for a moment, then seemed to grasp the situation. He reached into a compartment on his suit and pulled out a high-tech mask. With a swift motion, he placed it over his mouth and put the attached earplugs in each ear. The mask emitted a soft glow, and a small screen projected an electronic mouth onto the surface of the mask.

Ry-Lan spoke again. "Who are you? Why are you here?" The mask translated in a clear, male voice. It sounded like Ry-Lan but in English.

Alex took a deep breath. "My name is Alex. I'm from England. I met you a few years ago, and this," he gestured to the machine behind him, "is your machine."

Ry-Lan's eyes widened slightly, but his expression remained composed. "We must stop talking. We must not interfere with the flow of time. It destroys things," he said, the mask translating his words seamlessly.

Alex shook his head, his urgency clear. "I had to come because something bad will happen to you. I want to prevent it."

Ry-Lan's gaze sharpened. "If you tell me when I will die, time may interfere with me," he said, his tone unyielding.

"It's only just happened where I'm from," Alex insisted. "I can't see how it will break anything if I can prevent it."

Ry-Lan took a deep breath, considering Alex's words carefully. "You do not understand the complexity of time travel," he said finally. "Interference may have unpredictable consequences. Listen to me."

Alex was becoming upset. "I just want to help."

Ry-Lan glanced around, seriousness reflected in his eyes. "Listen carefully and follow my instructions. Deviation could be catastrophic."

Ry-Lan glanced at Alex, then pointed to a name on his uniform. "My name is *Ree-Lan*," he said, the translation mask ensuring clarity. "I am from year 2152. Part of group called observers. Travel through time to catalogue history."

Alex listened carefully, eyes widening with each revelation.

"We have crisis in our time," Ry-Lan continued. "Rampant disease threatens extinction. This crisis has changed our mandate. We seek new planet. And we travel to past to stop transmission of disease."

Alex's mind raced, trying to grasp the full implications. "So, you're here to stop this disease from spreading?"

"Yes," Ry-Lan confirmed. "Many people are dying. My team authorised to break gold rule. We identify chain of transmission and interfere it."

Ry-Lan paused, a look of regret crossing his face. "This moment, I know not much about chain or cause. I research it."

Alex hesitated but felt compelled to share. "I could tell you where you'll travel in the future; maybe it could help ..."

Ry-Lan's expression hardened. "No. Must not stop like that. I need your help now, but you must be careful. You must not act on the timeline of yourself. You must not interfere except to stop disease."

Ry-Lan went back into his machine and returned with a small card. "This card knows safe location. You travel to future to get help and instruction."

Alex took the card, examining it briefly. It looked like the machine access card, covered with writing and numbers. "What are you doing here in the USA?"

Ry-Lan shook his head. "No discuss more. I have job to do and little time to do it."

"But," Alex began.

"Go." Ry-Lan interrupted, his tone final. "Maybe meet again in the future."

Alex looked at Ry-Lan, determination and frustration in his eyes. "Alright. I'll do as you ask."

Ry-Lan turned back to his machine. Alex took a deep breath, turned, and returned to his own machine. As he initiated the return sequence, his mind raced about what he would tell Brian.

Thu 13th June

With a heavy heart and a mind brimming with new knowledge, Alex watched as the machine hummed back into existence at Bingley farm. The familiar surroundings did little to ease the burden of the revelations he carried. He stepped out, his breath steadying as he spotted Brian waiting near the barn, eyes filled with anticipation and concern.

Brian hurried over as Alex approached. "You're back. How did it go? What happened?"

Alex took a deep breath, trying to organise his thoughts. "It was … intense. I met Ry-Lan. Or rather, Ree Lan, as he calls himself."

Brian's eyes widened. "Ree Lan? What did he say?"

"He's from the year 2152. He is part of a group called the *Observers* who travel through time to document history, I think," Alex began, his voice loaded with the significance of the information. "But there's a crisis in his time — a disease threatening human extinction. They've been forced to change their mandate, and he has been sent back to investigate and, I think, to change the past to manage the disease's transmission."

Brian listened, his expression growing in severity. "So, he's here to stop this disease from spreading?"

"Yes," Alex confirmed, nodding slowly. "But on meeting him, he doesn't yet know much about the chain or how it is transmitted. He must be early in his mission."

Brian's concern deepened. "And what does that mean for us?"

"It means we have to be incredibly careful," Alex said, his voice firm. "Ree Lan gave me a card with a safe location where we can travel in the future for further help and instruction. He also clarified that we must not interact with ourselves in another timeline or interfere with anything unless it's essential to stop the disease."

Brian reached for the card, "Can I see it, please?"

Alex handed it to him, and Brian took photos of both sides of the card and carefully examined it. He used his translation app and then finally reported, "Emergency location. This card appears to be for emergency use."

"Yes, that's what I think Ree Lan was trying to tell me," agreed Alex. "Actually, can we just continue to call him 'Ry-Lan'? It just feels better."

"Sure. I know what you mean. Did Ry-Lan say anything about why he's in Washington?"

Alex shook his head. "He wouldn't discuss it. He said he had a job to do and was in a hurry. He told me to go home. Or maybe 'go here'. I'm not sure."

The significance of Ry-Lan's words created a tense silence. Brian placed a reassuring hand on Alex's shoulder. "We'll figure this out, Alex. We have to. For Ry-Lan's sake and everyone else."

Chapter 29

Alex suggested they go for a walk, hoping the beauty of the countryside might inspire them. Brian was happy for some fresh air. He appreciated why they kept the machine there, but he didn't particularly like the barn's dark interior.

Alex sighed. "So, where do we go from here? Ry-Lan gave us this card that contains like an emergency destination.

They walked in silence for a few minutes, both lost in thought. Finally, Alex broke the silence. "Let's go through what Ry-Lan has actually said to me. In Washington, he emphasised the importance of going to the future for assistance."

"Right," Brian replied. "And he was clear about not interfering with the past unless absolutely necessary. But he also wanted you to help with his mission, to defeat this disease that he talked of."

Alex kicked a small pebble off the path. "Yup. And then there was the Ry-Lan in the hospital. His message felt different. He seemed desperate like he wanted to tell us something more."

Brian looked up at the sky, squinting against the light. "Of course, Ry-Lan had already spent time investigating and visiting various locations after you saw him in Washington. Do you think he found something that influenced his message? Maybe he learned something critical that we don't know yet."

"That's possible," Alex said, frustration in his voice. "But without knowing the full context, it's hard to piece it all together."

Brian stopped walking and turned to face Alex. "We also have the video message that Ry-Lan recorded. What did he say? Family, water, disease?"

"He said a lot more than that, but that was all the doctor who helped us could understand."

"Do you think he wanted you to take that video to his people in the future? It could provide valuable information they need."

Alex's eyes lit up with realisation. "That would make sense. If we can show them the video, it might help them understand what's happening and how to stop the disease. Plus, he might also have the information they need on the machine."

Brian thought about this. "It's a bit risky but seems the best option. I don't see what else we have. Even if you travel and see Ry-Lan again, he'll probably refuse to talk to you."

Alex looked down at the card in his hand. "So, do you think you can use this card? You know, the coordinates on it? Can you programme the machine to get me there?"

"I think so. Yes. I recognise the coordinate format on the card. It's the same as the machine. But I don't think I need to enter it. I think the card can be inserted into the machine anyway. I've seen a space under the main screen where I think you can put cards. I'd tried the door card, but it didn't do anything. I've a feeling that this card will work there."

"OK, let's do it. Shall we do it now? I'm up for it. And if I don't go now, I'm worried I may not feel so brave later."

Brian placed a reassuring hand on Alex's shoulder. "I don't think that's such a good idea. A trip like this could be dangerous. I mean, they might have a lethal disease there even. You don't want to catch that or bring it back. What if that's what killed Ry-Lan?"

"If that killed Ry-Lan, then why have we not caught it yet?"

"OK, that's a good point, but we still need to be careful. There's too much at stake here. Maybe the whole future of the human race is resting in your hands."

Alex was convinced now. "Yes, when you put it like that ..."

They resumed their walk, the path winding through fields of tall grass swaying gently in the breeze. The tranquillity of the surroundings seemed at odds with the gravity of their conversation.

* * *

Alex and Brian decided to take a few days to mull over their options. The importance of their mission required careful thought, and they wanted to ensure they were making the right decision. They agreed to meet at Alex's house on Sunday to finalise their plans.

Alex had been about to end his shift at the station on the Friday afternoon when CI West called him into her office. His mood plummeted at the sound of her voice, stiff and formal as always.

"It's to do with the prank in Farmer Thompson's field that went wrong," she said, adjusting herself in her chair and peering at him over the rim of her glasses. "I am informed that the hospital consultant has referred Mr Ry-Lan's death to the coroner, who will be holding an inquest. You will be required to attend, and as your senior officer, I will be joining you."

Alex did his best to appear unperturbed. Although he'd been expecting it, this wasn't welcome news, right now.

"I see. When will ..."

"That's all the information I have. You'll be informed formally in due course," West said brusquely, waving him out.

As the days passed, Alex was distracted by the mounting pressure of their upcoming journey, eclipsing, for the time being, the coming inquest. He tried to take his mind off things by watching the Euro 2024 tournament that had just started, but every game only reminded him of his brother Mark. The matches were a bittersweet reminder of their shared passion for football and the complicated circumstances that now defined their relationship.

<u>Sun 16th June</u>

On Sunday morning, Alex prepared himself for their meeting. He paced the living room, running through everything in his mind. Just as he was lost in thought, the doorbell rang. He opened the door to find Brian standing there, looking determined.

"Morning, Alex. How have you been?" Brian asked as he stepped inside.

Alex shrugged, closing the door behind him. "I've been better, to be honest. This whole thing has been really getting to me."

Brian felt empathy for Alex. "I can imagine. Let's get the kettle on, and we can talk this through."

They headed to the kitchen, and Alex put the kettle on. As the water boiled, they sat at the table, the pressure of the conversation they were to have simmering away.

Brian started, "Are you sure you still want to do this, Alex? It's a big risk."

Alex took a deep breath. "I know it's risky, but we need answers. Ry-Lan gave us that card for a reason. We have to find out why."

Brian settled back in his chair, considering Alex's words. "Why do you think Ry-Lan gave us that destination? What was he trying to tell us?"

Alex stared at the kettle, deep in thought. "I think he wanted us to get help from his people. Maybe there's something in the future that can help us understand the disease and stop it. He seemed desperate, like he knew he couldn't do it alone."

"That makes sense. When he was in the hospital, you said he seemed to know you and gave you his card. That's pretty significant."

The kettle whistled, and Alex got up to make the tea. He brought the mugs back to the table, setting one in front of Brian. "I think we need to trust Ry-Lan. He knew the risks, but he still gave us that card, as you say. He must have wanted me to use it."

Brian sipped his tea, his expression serious. "You're right. We have to trust that he knew what he was doing. But you must still be cautious.

You'll be travelling to the year 2152. We have no idea what things will be like then."

Alex was keen to go. "Agreed. Let's finish our drinks and head off."

They sat silently for a moment, sipping their tea, the enormity of their decision sinking in. Then less than five minutes later, they were in Alex's car on the way to the farm.

Chapter 30

Within twenty minutes, Alex and Brian had arrived at Bingley farm. As they pulled up beside the barn, the atmosphere was thick with anticipation. Stepping out of the car, Alex glanced around, taking in the familiar surroundings.

They walked towards the barn, their footsteps crunching on the gravel. "This is it," Brian said, his voice low but steady. "You ready?"

Alex nodded, a resolute look in his eyes. "As ready as I'll ever be. Let's get everything set up."

Inside the barn, the machine stood waiting, an enigmatic portal to an uncertain future. Brian opened the machine and went inside. Alex stood behind him, watching intently. Brian was right about the slot. The card fitted neatly into it. When the card was inside, the display registered its presence by changing the screen to acknowledge the intended destination.

"Alright," Brian said, "the destination is set. That was pretty straightforward. Let's check the machine over."

Together, they examined each component, ensuring the machine was in order. They checked the power level, the outside cameras, and the integrity of the exterior, performing each step with extreme care. Once they were satisfied, Brian turned to Alex. "Everything looks good. Are you ready for this?"

Alex shook his head. "Not really. But let's get on with it before I back out."

Brian took a deep breath. "Okay, let's do this."

Alex stepped towards the machine, pausing for a moment to look back at Brian. "Thanks again, Brian. Whatever happens. I really appreciate it."

Brian smiled, pride and concern in his eyes. "Don't talk like that. You'll be back again before you know it. Well, before I know it, anyway."

With a final smile, Alex stepped into the machine. He slid into the seat, looked at the display, and breathed deeply. Strapping himself in, he closed the hatch.

Brian stood near the entrance. "Good luck, Alex. See you soon."

The machine whirred to life. Alex experienced an adrenaline rush as the machine began to vibrate, the sensation intensifying as the countdown gathered pace. In an instant, the world as he knew it was gone, to be replaced by the promise of the future.

* * *

Alex felt the machine stop, the vibrations ceasing and the whirlwind of light fading away. His heart thundered as he activated the external cameras. He seemed to be in a large room, possibly a lab or studio, deserted nonetheless.

He unstrapped himself and cautiously stepped out of the machine. The world he stepped into was both familiar and alien. For a couple of minutes, he was alone there. He could see the room better now. He looked up. Where he thought the ceiling would be, he could see the sky. Or was it? It looked like the sky, but at about ten metres high, the wall adjoined what now seemed to be a ceiling of glass or some display. He couldn't be sure.

The various machines and equipment reminded him of what one might see in a hangar or a garage. A wheeled flight of steps and an inspection pit were nearby. A couple of figures stood on one side of the room in human form but were wearing armour, not clothes, and their eyes were closed as if asleep. As he approached them, one of the figures woke up and began walking towards him. The figure appeared neither male nor female. They resembled an adult-sized prepubescent boy with closely cropped hair. They spoke to Alex in a language similar to Ry-Lan's. Their voice was kind and gentle, sing-song in nature, like a love song.

Alex spoke to the man-boy, "My name is Alex. Who are you?"

The man-boy closed his eyes and, after reopening them, spoke to Alex in English, "Welcome. I am An Zhou Shi. How can I help you?"

Alex spoke again, "My name is Alex. Who or what are you?" He immediately regretted his clumsy choice of words.

"Welcome, Alex. I am a helper. How may I help you today?"

"Where am I?" Alex asked, frowning and looking around.

"You are in reception area three."

Alex wanted to know so much, but strangely, words escaped him. He regretted not making a list of things to find out. Just when he was about to form another question, the helper closed, reopened his eyes, and spoke again, "Who are you?"

Alex felt a sense of déjà vu, "My name is Alex Harper. Where is everyone?"

"I am Commander Kwi Kwang. Where are you from? Why are you here?"

Alex swallowed, finding his situation inhibiting and struggling to respond adequately. "I am from England, from the year 2024. I met your colleague, Ry-Lan. I mean Ree Lan. This is his machine. He asked me to deliver you a message. I have a recording from him to share with you."

The helper said nothing. It just stared at Alex. Then, it closed and reopened its eyes once more. "Please follow me. I will take you to a greeting room. Would you like any refreshments?"

"No, I'm fine, thank you." Alex followed the helper as they left the room, and the helper navigated a series of corridors. At the end of the corridors, they entered an elevator and, after exiting, went into a nearby room.

The room was small. It had what looked like a window across its centre, occupying its full height and width. Sets of tables and chairs stood on both sides of the window. Alex felt that he was supposed to sit down. The helper stood against the wall next to the door.

Soon after Alex had sat down, a man entered the room on the other side of the glass. He sat down, too, and stared at Alex.

He was clearly a tall man with a military poise that Alex recognised from his brother. The man had a full head of silver hair and an unmistakable air of authority.

As the man spoke, a voice came from above Alex in English. "I greet you, Alex. I am Commander Kwi Kwang. Please explain your purpose."

Alex took a deep breath. "Thank you. My name is Alex, and I'm from the year 2024. I was sent here by Ree-Lan. He told me that your world is facing a crisis with an infectious disease. He recorded a video that he wanted me to give to you."

The man listened intently, his expression serious. The commander spoke again. Clearly, his voice was being translated because Alex saw his mouth move before he heard the voice. "We know Ree Lan. Put the video on tray."

The commander indicated a smooth panel on the table, and Alex instinctively put his phone on the panel. The man looked at the phone and then back at Alex. "Where is video?"

Alex picked up the phone and started to play the video. He held up the phone next to the glass so the man could see it. The commander seemed surprised. He watched the video closely. "Again. Louder."

Alex turned up the volume on his phone and played it again. To Alex's surprise, the man stood up and left the room. Alex waited. He looked at his watch. It said 11:25 a.m. He was trying to work out what time he had left the farm when the door behind him opened, and a woman in what looked like a hazmat suit came in. She held her hand in front of her face and spoke to it in her language. The helper next to the door stepped forward and opened their eyes. The woman spoke again, and the helper translated her words, "I greet you. My name is Bei He."

Alex stood and bowed slightly to the woman. He saw her face. Even through the suit, he could see that she was beautiful. He could not determine her age. Perhaps she was around 30. He responded clumsily, "Hello. I am Alex. I am from England."

"Yes, I know you," she replied with a smile. "Follow me, please."

Bei He left the room with the helper immediately behind her. Alex followed, too, as they made their way into the elevator. The woman spoke, and the elevator appeared to ascend. As they exited, Alex recognised the corridors from earlier.

"Follow me, please," Bei He said again through the bot.

Alex did as he was told. Before too long, they were back in the room where he had begun this part of his journey. Or at least so he thought. As he looked around, he realised it was different from where he had landed. Bei He walked over to the sphere in the centre, placed her hand on the side of the machine, and the hatch opened.

"Go in," she said, pointing. "Sit down."

Alex understood what she wanted, got into the machine, and sat in the chair. He buckled up as before. The woman got into the machine also. Leaving the helper outside, she operated the interface to close the hatch. She continued to operate the machine with the skill and ability of someone clearly very familiar with it.

Alex recognised the familiar timer on the screen and knew she had initiated the jump sequence. As the time approached zero, Bei He stood with her legs between Alex's and gripped his chair's headrest with both hands.

Moments later, the vibrations ceased, signalling their arrival back in the present. He glanced at Bei He, who stood calmly, ready for what would come next.

"We're here," Alex said, unbuckling himself and standing up. He gestured towards the hatch. "Let's get out, and you can meet my friend Brian, too."

Bei He clearly didn't understand what Alex was saying. Then Alex realised they had left the translation helper droid behind. He indicated the hatch.

Bei He operated the hatch opening, and Alex slid past her and stepped out of the machine. He put his hand back in a gesture for her to follow. But instead of following, she closed the hatch again.

"Hey!" Alex called. "What are you doing?"

Alex scrambled in his pockets and dug out the access card. He held it against the panel they used to open the machine. Nothing happened. He presented it again. Still nothing.

Brian called out, "Alex, what's happening?"

Alex turned to face Brian, but he couldn't find his words. He stuttered, "I ... I ... she ..."

He turned back to look at the machine again, but it was gone. Alex stood in stunned silence, staring at the space where the machine had been.

"I don't know, Brian," Alex said with frustration and confusion. "It looks like they tricked me. The people from the future have taken the machine back."

Brian put a reassuring hand on Alex's shoulder. "We need a brew. Come and tell me what happened."

Brian turned and strode out of the barn towards Alex's car. Brian opened the boot and took his flask from his rucksack. He poured two cups and waited for Alex to join him.

"I thought she wanted to help," Alex said, shaking his head. "But then she just took the machine and left."

Brian frowned. "Maybe they have their reasons for taking the machine back. But at least they got you back safely."

Alex glanced up at the heavens, shrugged, and, reaching into his pocket, pulled out the access card Ry-Lan gave him. "I guess all I have left is this. A souvenir from our travels. You can have it."

Brian examined the card and then handed it back to Alex, "Maybe we're not done yet. Strange things happen. Aren't we testimony to that? Just put it somewhere safe."

- The End -

Hi. Did you enjoy reading this novel? I hope so. Would you like to see a sequel? And maybe even suggest ideas for what to include in it?

Perhaps like me, you have been captivated by the idea of time travel since childhood. Maybe you've wondered, if you could travel in time then what would you do? Where would you want to go? Would you try to see events in your own past, perhaps even give yourself advice? Or would you be a "time tourist" and travel to famous events throughout history? Or would you want to see the future?

When writing this novel, I have intentionally left "hooks" in the plot to allow for a sequel. Did you see them? Can you work out which character(s) will travel next?

I have a rough outline for the next story in the sequence, but it is only a draft, and I am open to other ideas about what might happen next. After all, most of the characters in the story are just ordinary people like you and me, so they could easily want to do the same things that we might want to. And the concept of the story gives infinite potential really for exploration, especially since the machine can also travel in space as well as time.

So please, reach out to me at alex@ry-lan.com with any suggestions that you might have. I'm not promising to use them, but maybe you can help to shape a future storyline in the series.

Thanks
Alex

Printed in Dunstable, United Kingdom